Memories Made at Midnight

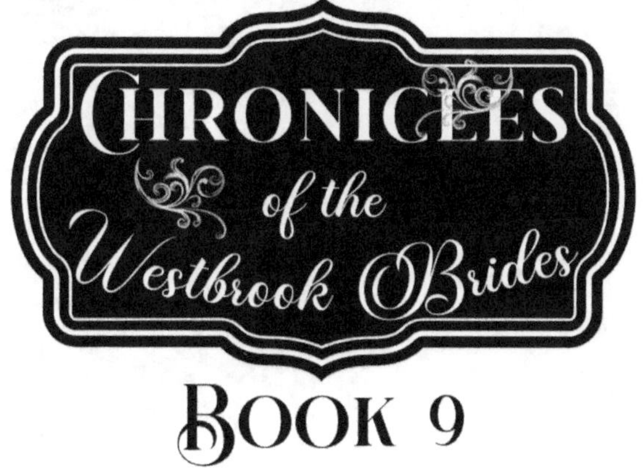

Chronicles of the Westbrook Brides

Book 9

Blue Rose Romance® LLC

transmitted in any form or by any electronic or mechanical means, including photocopying, recording, or by any information storage and retrieval system, without the written permission of the publisher, except where permitted by law.

NO AI TRAINING: Without in any way limiting the author's [and publisher's] exclusive rights under copyright, any use of this publication to "train" generative artificial intelligence (AI) technologies to generate text is **expressly prohibited**. The author reserves all rights to license uses of this work for generative AI training and development of machine learning language models.

For permission requests, write to the publisher at the address below.

Attn: Permissions Coordinator

Blue Rose Romance® LLC

PO Box 167

Scappoose, Oregon 97056 USA

collettecameron.com

eBook ISBN: 978-1-955259-59-0

Print Book ISBN: 978-1-955259-61-3

Cassius wrapped his arms around her quaking form, whispering soothing words into her silky hair.

I'm lost.
Utterly and
irreversibly lost.

Regardless, Beatrice
would never know.
Because he'd taken an oath
to never love again, and his
word was his bond.

GET YOUR FREE BOOK!

JOIN MY EXCLUSIVE MAILING LIST
AND GET A FREE EBOOK!

Plus Sneak Peeks, Giveaways, Contests,
Exclusive Content and More...
P.S. I promise only good stuff ~ no spammy stuff!

Scan the following QR Code to join
The Regency Rose VIP Group Mailing List
and get your FREE BOOK!

Thank you,
Collette Cameron®

THE REGENCY ROSE®
VIP CLUB

PRAISE FOR...
COLLETTE CAMERON®

See What Readers Are Saying About
Collette Cameron®

★★★★★ "...a fast and delightful read with plenty of heart and humor."

— BOOKWORM 2 BOOKWORM

★★★★★ "Collette Cameron has an amazing skill with historical romances."

— NIGHT OWL REVIEWS

★★★★★ "Cameron conveys the tone of the Regency era well... highlights for the reader how far we've come as women in society..."

— RABID READERS REVIEWS

MEMORIES MADE AT MIDNIGHT

A ROMANTIC OPPOSITES ATTRACT MYSTERY & SUSPENSE FAMILY SAGA REGENCY ROMANCE

CHRONICLES OF THE WESTBROOK BRIDES
BOOK NINE

COLLETTE CAMERON®

*For my dogs, Pebbles and Ayva, who
always listen politely to my plot ideas.*

ONE

Highbury House
Home of the estimable but dour
Earl of Highbury
Brighton, England

AUGUST 1828 ~ EARLY MORNING

Something doesn't feel right...

Singing *Greensleeves* softly to herself, Beatrice Fairfax casually glanced around as she wandered across the lawn toward her private sanctuary like she did every morning before breaking her fast.

Nothing appeared out of the ordinary, and yet...

Something felt off, as if the day portended unexpected or unpleasant happenings.

A shudder skittered up her spine, and she squinted toward the house.

Yes.

There on the first floor.

Uncle stood before the mullioned study window, observing her, his expression unreadable at this distance.

How peculiar.

He rarely rose before ten.

What prompted him to do so today?

As if sensing her perusal, Uncle Cedric spun away and disappeared from view.

God only knew what motivated Cedric Fairfax, Earl of Highbury?

Beatrice had given up trying to understand or please him long ago.

Accompanied by her two canine shadows—Nala, the badly beaten boarhound Beatrice had rescued two years ago from a drunken sailor and who now weighed more than Beatrice, and tiny Teddy, the blind-in-one-eye, starving black Pekingese runt she'd found wandering Brighton's streets a few months before that—Beatrice resumed her short trek to what once had been the carriage house.

Several years ago, Uncle Cedric had commissioned a larger, more extravagant structure for his five conveyances which housed his horseflesh too.

Waiting for her as he did every morning, Hans, the

cook's grandson, waved. The boy adored helping Beatrice with the animals and wanted to explore the new field of veterinary medicine.

At present, only a few animals called the pretty little structure their home. With several outer cages and fencing surrounding the building on two sides, the sanctuary had also served as a makeshift hospital for many other unfortunate creatures over the years.

An involuntary sigh escaped Beatrice.

If only women could become animal doctors. The vocation greatly appealed to her.

They couldn't, of course.

Most especially not an earl's niece.

Regardless, that didn't stop Beatrice from reading everything she could get her hands on about treating animals, including *The Veterinarian's Vade Mecum*, *The Complete Grazier*, and *A Treatise on the Disease of Horses*. Maybe someday, women would have the same opportunities and liberties as men, but that day most assuredly was not today.

And unquestionably would not occur in the foreseeable future.

Not if Uncle Cedric and other stodgy peers had their imperious way.

Fortunately, Beatrice had the means to rescue wounded and abandoned animals and nurse them back to health. Those who could survive and thrive on their own, she released into the wild. The rest became dear friends and companions, every bit as loyal as Esme Dawkins and Charlotte Hawthorne.

Esme, the eldest daughter of Reverend Ellison Dawkins, the vicar of St. Nicholas Church, and Charlotte, the only granddaughter to widowed Mrs. Clementine Halsey, didn't care about Beatrice's occasional stutter. Nor did they judge her about being born on the wrong side of the blanket, something she had no control over. Their unconditional acceptance and love kept her stoic and determined. They even helped with her menagerie from time to time.

Unlike Uncle Cedric.

The haughty curmudgeon disapproved of Beatrice's interest in nursing animals.

In truth, he disliked everything about her: that she was his sister's illegitimate daughter, Beatrice's tendency to stumble over her words when she felt anxious or nervous, her *shocking* hair color, (his critical opinion, not anyone else's), her lack of suitors, and mostly her imposition upon his bachelor lifestyle these past two decades.

Even her name, Beatrice Blossom Carina Fairfax, vexed him—particularly her middle name, Carina. As her uncle had pointed out time and again, her mother's affair with a married Italian man was scandalous enough. But giving Beatrice an Italian middle name that meant 'beloved' only added insult to injury.

Uncle Cedric's long nose twitched, and his once handsome features became even more stern whenever Beatrice's friends addressed her by her nickname, *BeBe*.

'Twas what Mama had called her, and Beatrice didn't give two flicks of a lamb's tail if it annoyed her uncle into apoplexy. She would not give up the moniker. In that small way, she rebelled against his inflexible strictures. However, in her mind, a riot of recalcitrant thoughts, entirely unbefitting a docile, biddable young woman, tumbled continually about.

How shocked and appalled would Uncle Cedric be if he had any notion of her mutinous musings?

It was a small wonder he permitted Beatrice her pets. But then again, her animals kept her occupied, and away from the social events they received invitations to.

She was no fool.

Beatrice knew full well her name on an invitation was obligatory, not a genuine desire for her presence. She was an *undesirable* from her birth, to her unpopular coloring in a world of golden blondes and sable brunettes—not to mention her propensity for clumsiness.

Tending her animals also meant she wasn't in the house and underfoot, exasperating Uncle Cedric at every turn. And as she used her allowance from her trust fund to finance her *little hobby,* as he called it, he couldn't squabble about the expense of her venture, either.

Only two and a half more years—when Beatrice

reached her fifth and twentieth birthday—and the bulk of her inheritance would be hers. She could—*and would, by Jove*—leave her stern and unloving uncle's house. At last, she would be free of his censure, dark glowers, cutting retorts, and haughty disdain.

As a child, his callousness and contempt had frightened and discouraged Beatrice. She tried—desperately and pathetically—to earn a smile or a kind word. However, she'd long since stopped trying to gain his approval—an impossibility because of her mere existence, and she'd come to accept that fact without rancor.

In truth, she was past the age of majority, and at two and twenty, she *could* leave Highbury House now. But how did a respectable woman with few useful talents (even fewer that made her employable) and a lack of available funds, survive in a world which required both until she came into her inheritance?

No, Beatrice would continue to bide her time and steer clear of Uncle Cedric as much as possible, ignore his ever-increasing frequent and bold suggestions that she should marry (men weren't exactly lining up to court her), and plan for the day when she was free to make her own decisions.

A refreshing breeze bearing the faintest tangy tinge of the sea caressed Beatrice's face and bare arms. The mild wind flirted with the few remaining purple crepe myrtle blossoms and Persian silk pink pom-poms.

Beatrice had eschewed a bonnet and shawl in favor of soaking in a few glorious rays of sunshine. Soon enough, England's gray, dank, and cold autumn and winter would be upon the coastal township and she would be glad she had indulged herself.

How she longed to travel to milder, warmer climes.

She lifted her face skyward—half in defiance and half in satisfaction.

What were a few more freckles?

Besides her strawberry-blonde hair—far more berry than blonde—nature had seen fit to pepper her body and face with reddish-brown spots. How cruel the other girls at school had been, poking fun at her freckles, pretending they might catch a disease from her.

Lifting her boxy nose, Nala sniffed the air.

Fluffy ears raised, Teddy followed suit before issuing a single *woof*.

The dogs sensed it too—something *was* afoot.

But what?

Tingles zipped up Beatrice's back.

Every warning instinct she possessed silently screeched within her.

Caution. Danger. Peril.

TWO

❦

Still in Highbury House's gardens

HALF A DOZEN FRENZIED HEARTBEATS LATER

Slowing her pace, Beatrice scanned the landscape and rubbed her arms to dispel the gooseflesh that had arisen there.

Other than a pair of turtle doves soaring toward a horse chestnut tree, nothing disturbed the morning's tranquility. A lone, pristine white cloud floated in the cerulean sky. A ten-foot weather-worn stone wall encased the estate, assuring that no vagrants or uninvited visitors could enter the earl's immaculately tended property.

"It's all right," she assured the dogs, although she wasn't positive everything *was* all right.

Nala gently nudged Teddy's nose and received a wet tongue across her muzzle in response.

Perhaps having both experienced abuse and deprivation, the two dogs had become inseparable, besides being Beatrice's most ardent protectors. She could walk nearly everywhere in Brighton with only the dogs as her chaperones—which she did at every opportunity, despite her uncle's disapproval, though he hadn't forbidden her jaunts.

After all, what was he to do?

Accompany her or prohibit her sojourns and bear her presence all the more?

No, permitting her to roam at will was the lesser of the evils, and how she relished that small jot of freedom.

With her faithful dogs at her side, no one dared so much as glance in her direction without the appropriate degree of respect awarded to the Earl of Highbury's niece.

With another small sigh, Beatrice surveyed the lavish grounds.

Golden sunlight bathed the tidy verdant lawns, neat-as-a-pin hedgerows, the dual rows of meticulously tended roses, and the ostentatious five-story manor painted a pleasant ivory shade.

Elegant stone Grecian urns brimming with trailing ivy and seasonal flowers, including regal orange, pink, red, and yellow begonias, nasturtiums, and pink and purple petunias—a rather new bloom to England—adorned the terrace on the house's west-facing side.

The continuous muffled roar of the waves breaking along the shore echoed in the distance, harmonizing with the ever-present, ringing cries of gulls.

How Beatrice loved those comforting sounds. She always wanted to live near the sea. But not in Brighton, where she might encounter her taciturn uncle.

Filling her lungs with balmy air, she closed her eyes and willed her topsy-turvy stomach to settle. The house and grounds, while beautiful, were nothing but a façade, an elegant veneer presented to the public, hiding the dysfunction within.

Hans bobbed his blond head as he patted Nala's back.

"Morning, Miss Beatrice."

"Good morning, Hans."

He opened the door, and Beatrice slipped into the carriage house, Nala and Teddy on her heels.

Fabian, a three-legged fox, missing half an ear and blind in one eye, lifted his head and gave her a foxy smile before burying his face in his bushy, russet tail once more. He'd spend this afternoon outdoors in the long run, built on one side of the carriage house.

"Can I feed Fabian today?" Hans gazed at the fox with adoration.

"Of course you can."

Sporting a wide grin, the boy hurried to the shelf where Beatrice kept Fabian's food—mostly leftovers the boy's kind-hearted grandmother saved for the animals.

Monty, a hare Beatrice had rescued from a snare, hopped with a lopsided gait to the side of his cage to greet her. Isabella, a dove with a broken wing who would never fly again, but who spent her mornings in an aviary when the weather permitted it, cooed softly.

Deaf and blind after two bratty youths had tried to drown him, Lancelot, the ugliest cat Beatrice had ever seen, unfolded from his feline coil and unerringly found his way to her despite his sensory deficiencies.

Laughter bubbled up from her chest at the warm greetings from her animal friends.

Hans chuckled while petting the contented fox, happily munching away on a meaty bone. The lad knew the daily routine so well he could care for her pets by himself if needed.

Mewing softly, Lancelot wound between her ankles before nudging noses with both dogs. Despite her massive size, Nala remained unerringly gentle with the smaller creatures.

"I know you're hungry, my dears. I shall hurry."

After securing an apron over her simple but pretty yellow gingham frock, Beatrice set about tending to her charges.

Beatrice resumed singing as she completed her daily chores, allowing her mind to wander to a time when she'd be free of this gilded prison. Except for eight extremely painful years spent in boarding and finishing schools, awful, humiliating experiences she preferred to put from her mind, Beatrice had never left Brighton.

She fully intended to rectify that once she gained her freedom.

Naturally, Nala and Teddy would accompany her. As for her other pets, she planned on hiring someone to care for them while she traveled from one splendid, *warm* location to another.

Surely, if she economized, dedicated herself to thriftiness, and invested wisely, her inheritance could sustain her throughout her life.

Wrinkling her forehead, she paused in sweeping the floor.

When the time came, she needed to find someone reliable and honest to help her invest her inheritance.

But who?

Would Reverend Dawkins know of anyone?

It couldn't hurt to ask, but there was no rush. Neither was there any harm in educating herself on the matter, so that when she came into her inheritance, she would be prepared.

The door swung open, and she barely suppressed a gasp.

Once more, warning bells clanged louder than Notre Dame Cathedral's.

Uncle stood silhouetted in the opening.

This couldn't bode well.

Even at seven and forty, he presented a fine figure of manhood. Tall and slender, he turned many a woman's head. Regardless, he gave no female more than a passing glance. He spent far more time on his toilet and appearance than Beatrice ever had, and she thought him a rather vain man.

Only once before had he ventured into Beatrice's private domain.

Mouth turned down in disapproval, he raked his steely gaze over her, Hans, and the animals.

When had he ever spared her a kind word or a smile?

Hans sent her a nervous glance before edging toward the doorway. "I'll see you this evening, Miss."

Uncle stepped aside, and the child darted out, making good his escape.

Lucky soul.

Without preamble, Uncle Cedric announced, "I've arranged to have an artist paint a miniature of you, Beatrice. I've also purchased a gown worthy of your station for you to wear and have directed Millborn to style your hair."

He gestured toward his own neatly combed, rich brown locks, distinguished gray peppering his temples.

"You shall wear my mother's emerald and diamond parure set. I expect you to be ready at half of three when the artist arrives."

As was his wont, Uncle Cedric gave orders. Never once had he inquired about what Beatrice might want or prefer.

Head canted, she tried to calm the trepidation storming inside her as she wiped her hands on her apron.

"What n-need is there for me t-to have a m-miniature painted?"

She didn't fool herself into believing it was because he wanted a token to remember her by.

No, this unfeeling, cold-hearted man had rid the house of every single remnant of his sister when she'd run away with the Italian lace merchant who later broke her heart and left her with child. To this day, Uncle Cedric refused to speak Mama's name, referring to her as "your mother" or "my sister."

"It's enough that I decree it, Niece," he snapped.

His features shifted, and something akin to chagrin flitted across his stern visage, but the impression was so fleeting that Beatrice thought she must have imagined it.

He stepped outside and in his usual unapologetic and arrogant air said, "I've decided it's past time you marry, Beatrice. I mean to travel to London with the miniature to assure potential suitors that you are not entirely unbecoming. Once a match has been arranged, you shall exchange vows in London as well."

"M-m-marry?"

Please, God.

He cannot be serious.

Would Beatrice's husband take possession of her money?

She'd never seen the will or trust documents. Neither did she know if her inheritance remained under her control after marriage.

If they did not...

Beatrice would be in exactly the same position as now.

No, far, *far* worse.

Marriage was for a lifetime. She'd have no hope of escape.

"With your grandmother's inheritance as enticement, even your stutter and lack of social graces might be overlooked, and an acceptable match is not beyond hope." He flicked a piece of lint off his expensively tailored jacket.

He might've requested the butler refold his news sheets, so disinterested did he sound.

Beatrice clasped her hands together until her fingertips grew numb. "Am I t-to have n-no choice in t-the m-matter?"

God, how she hated her stutter, especially when she needed to speak her mind.

"Of course, you have a choice." His flinty, gray,

emotionless gaze pierced her as he slid his mouth upward an inch into a predatory smile. "You are free to refuse my decree. However, if you do so, I shall put you from my house at once. I've more than met my obligation to your mother."

Am I to exchange one prison for another?

THREE

Sussex Square-Kempton
Brighton, England

AUGUST 1828 ~ QUARTER TO NOON

Paintbrush and palette in hand, Cassius Westbrook retreated six paces, and head cocked, examined the stormy seascape he'd been working on with a critical eye. The lighting still wasn't quite right. It didn't capture the power and majesty of the churning ocean and wrathful sky at dawn.

He swung his attention to the large window looking out onto the glittering Atlantic Ocean. This summer day, the waves caressed the pebbled shoreline rather than angrily bludgeoning the beach, and the clear azure sky soothed the spirit rather than stirring dread.

Sighing, he slid the paintbrush into a jar of turpentine.

The painting would have to await his return. Landscapes and genre art were his passion, but commissioned portraits, sketches, and the occasional holy painting for a chapel or church paid his bills.

Not that he didn't enjoy painting portraits, for he did.

However, portraits were meant to leave a lasting, positive impression. Those sitting for the reproduction of their likenesses wore their finest clothing and jewels, made certain not a hair was out of place, arranged their features into pleasant miens, and chose flattering settings to enhance their likeness and preserve their immortality.

Genre paintings, illustrating scenes and individuals from daily life, captured humanity in its true form—be it beautiful, unattractive, magnificent, impoverished, joyful, or sorrowful. These compositions offered an endless variety of subjects, freezing a moment in history for future generations to explore, analyze, learn from, and appreciate.

After Constanza's betrayal, he'd honestly feared he'd never be able to paint again, but a few months ago, the desire to create came roaring back with a vengeance.

Thank God, for he didn't know what he'd have done with his life if he couldn't be an artist.

He slipped off his paint-stained smock, and after hanging it on a nearby hook, gave the stormy seascape a final critical glance. Tomorrow morning, he'd give it another go. With a shrug, he scratched his nose and made for his bedchamber upstairs.

Passing through his studio, he roved his gaze over the dozen or so finished paintings.

He needed twenty for the show scheduled in London next spring.

A show Cassius was certain his father had arranged via his many influential connections, even though Cassius had told the duke time and again, that he wanted to earn his success on his merit.

However, Father had reminded Cassius that he was but one of five young artists featured, and the committee had made the selections without the Duke of Latham's influence. Cassius still wasn't convinced that was truly the case. Nonetheless, he wasn't foolish enough to refuse the exposure the British Institution would provide him.

As he ascended the time-worn stairs, he unbuttoned his shirt and reflected on his life in Brighton these past several months.

A duke's younger sons rarely had the opportunity to earn a satisfactory living while pursuing their passions. But then, his parents, the Duke and Duchess of Latham, weren't typical aristocrats either. They'd always encouraged their eight children to pursue their dreams, even if Society frowned upon their unconventional choices.

Just two months ago, his twin Darius had celebrated the grand opening of his bookstore in Woodhaven. Fletcher, one of Cassius's older half-brothers, owned two clubs and a theater in London. Leonidas traveled the world. Lucius worked as a private investigator after years of spying for His Majesty. Adolphus—the future duke— operated a shipping enterprise, and Althelia, the only sister among the Westbrook siblings, could out-shoot and outride all the brothers.

Each of those bacon-brained siblings had fallen in love too.

Only he and Layton, the other half-brother and most recently of His Majesty's Army, remained unfettered by marital obligations. Layton's disinterest in matrimony stemmed from an unfaithful wife over a decade before. He'd sworn off women for life.

Cassius's dreams had taken him to Italy to train under Vincenzo Camuccini, and he'd become great friends with Francesco Hayez who, in Cassius's opinion, would become a leader in Italian Romanticism.

He'd also fallen in love with Constanza Segreti, the daughter of the man Cassius had rented his small, but quaint villa from. They became betrothed, and he convinced himself that God smiled down upon him. His two greatest passions were within reach—marriage to a woman he cherished and recognition as an accomplished artist.

Until sloe-eyed Constanza tossed him aside for a more affluent man.

Why would she want to marry the youngest son of a duke, scraping by on his commissions when she could become the wife of a prestigious and wealthy local gentleman?

Cassius had been a stupid, gullible fool once.

He'd never give his heart again.

In that, he very much understood Layton's stance on romance.

Firming his mouth, Cassius shook off his melancholy musings as he glided his hand up the smooth handrail. The past was the past. He couldn't change a bloody, buggering thing about it, nor did he want to.

He'd learned a valuable lesson and was free to dedicate the remainder of his life to his art without the encumbrances and demands of a wife. As for children...Well, with seven siblings, surely, he would have several nieces and nephews to dote upon. Besides, it wasn't as if Father relied upon him as an heir.

Luck was with him the day he'd stumbled upon these accommodations. In the up-and-coming Kempton neighborhood, his house had once been a millinery and dressmaking establishment catering to Brighton's *haut ton* elite and owned by the three spinster Stitchwell sisters.

Cassius strongly suspected Stitchwell was not their actual surname.

When the eldest sister, suddenly and unexpectedly passed, the two remaining sisters sold their shop and decided to spend the remainder of their years doing whatever they blasted well pleased.

That was the way to live life.

Each day felt like a rare treasure that would not come again.

Once Cassius had donned a cream and charcoal striped waistcoat, he expertly tied a pale gray neckcloth into a mail coach knot, then slipped on a dove-colored jacket. He examined himself in the cheval mirror.

Tasteful and reserved, but not severe and unapproachable.

Appropriate for a noble-born portraitist, but his attire didn't scream privilege.

His lineage wasn't a secret in Brighton; however, Cassius preferred to gain clients on his worth, not Father's influence and station.

Swiping his dark hair with a boar-bristle brush, he considered today's patron.

Lord Highbury was a peculiar chap.

An acquaintance of Father's, his lordship had sought Cassius and commissioned him to paint a miniature of his niece, offering to pay him double his usual portrait fee.

"I've heard good things about you, Westbrook, though why a noble with your estimable lineage would choose to work, I cannot fathom."

Of course, the likes of Highbury couldn't.

Work was beneath nobles and aristocrats who believed themselves superior to commoners.

Cassius had quirked an eyebrow, already disliking the pretentious bore. "Oh?"

"Indeed." Highbury had nodded, not quite able to keep the disdain from his expression.

As if Cassius cared one whit what the pompous prig thought of him. Still, Highbury was a generous patron, and Cassius had a mortgage to pay, for he refused to accept any financial support from his father.

"No one would ever mistake my niece for a diamond of the first water or a fine English rose." Highbury had shaken his head, his tight expression suggesting he'd either sucked a lemon or passed wind. "Regardless, Beatrice's youth and inheritance ought to entice a desperate chap or two. Her figure is also passable, I suppose."

So the rotter wasn't even dowering her, and he'd spoken of her as if she were cattle.

Cassius had almost asked if the earl had inspected her teeth.

Highbury had clasped his lapels, while gazing condescendingly around Cassius's studio, before curling his upper lip. "She's part Italian, but you'd never know it with that garish red hair of hers. Still, I'm confident with your skill you can create a flattering likeness."

Interesting.

Beatrice Fairfax had red hair.

Coppery red?

Strawberry-blonde?

Flaming orange, chestnut, or auburn?

"Might I ask why you wish me to paint a miniature?" With his forefinger, Cassius had nudged a painting of a seaside café upward on one side. "I normally only paint full-sized portraits."

"I mean to marry the chit off as expeditiously as possible." Highbury had smiled, a thin, cunning upward sweep of his mouth, reminding Cassius of a fox with a hen in its jaws. "Her mother saddled me with her, and Beatrice has been a burden for two decades. I'll hie to London with the miniature and arrange a marriage for her, posthaste."

He didn't need a portrait to arrange a marriage.

Upon learning Highbury's distasteful intentions, Cassius had almost refused the commission, but something—mayhap curiosity about the young woman Highbury was so desperate to be rid of—prompted him to accept.

"More fool me," Cassius muttered as he climbed into the curricle several minutes later. Guilt for his part in the poor girl's fate pricked him during the ten-minute drive to Highbury House.

You could always refuse to paint the miniature.

True, Cassius could, but Highbury would merely find another willing artist.

As he descended the curricle, Cassius came to a conclusion.

I'll wait until I meet the girl to make a final decision.

FOUR

Highbury House Gardens

Barely able to keep a mutinous scowl from forming, Beatrice held her head high as she clasped the yards and yards of seafoam green silk in her white-gloved hands and traversed the terrace flagstones. With each step, she held her breath so she wouldn't trip over the fabric and make a fool of herself, yet again.

She grudgingly admitted that the sophisticated young woman who'd stared back at her in the oval cheval mirror in her chamber bore little resemblance to the girl attired in a gingham frock that morning.

Millborn had swept Beatrice's hair into a confection of curls, leaving a few tresses to trail down to her left shoulder. The servant intertwined a creamy satin ribbon through the strawberry-blonde locks before tucking two jeweled emerald combs into the coiffure. The emeralds at Beatrice's ears and throat twinkled happily in her reflection, oblivious to the turmoil inside the solemn-eyed woman who wore them.

Then, at Uncle's insistence, the kindly maid had set about applying cosmetics to Beatrice's face, which did rather enhance her features nicely. The rice powder muted her freckles and gave her complexion a creamy appearance. The lip and cheek rouge added spots of color to her pale skin, and her gold-tipped lashes appeared ever so much thicker and darker with the light application of burned cork paste.

Beatrice pondered the use of cosmetics, generally reserved for and associated with women of loose morals. Uncle must be quite desperate to make her more appealing, which only cast additional self-doubt upon her already bruised esteem.

For as long as she could remember, Uncle Cedric had told her how unattractive she was.

From what faint memories she had of her sweet mother, Mama had been beautiful.

Beatrice permitted her mouth to turn downward as she descended the wide stone stairway.

All the rest of the morning and into the afternoon, Beatrice had fumed about Uncle Cedric's audacity. Over and over, she'd tried to create a scenario that wouldn't require her to marry a stranger—probably a decrepit old sod reeking of garlic and dirty feet—or render her homeless without a farthing.

She had considered—for all of three seconds—asking Uncle to allow her to borrow against her trust and set up a modest house elsewhere or to loan her the money to do so, which she would repay promptly upon turning five and twenty.

However, she strongly suspected his acrimony toward her wouldn't permit him to show her that kindness or favor and had quickly discarded those hair-brained notions.

She'd only agreed to sit for the dratted portrait to buy herself a little more desperately needed time.

Surely it would take Uncle a few weeks to find a gentleman who agreed to marry her, sight unseen. Well, not precisely sight unseen. There would be the miniature portrait, after all.

If the artist ever finished the likeness.

And that was precisely when the beginnings of a plan started to hatch.

Beatrice could delay the painting's completion.

Yes, indeed.

Just the thing.

Beatrice Blossom Carina Fairfax, you've become devious.

She glanced downward, only a smidgeon of remorse sluicing through her for what she was about to do to this lovely gown. For she had just determined that mishap after mishap would occur to prevent the artist from completing the miniature in a timely fashion.

The truth of it was, Beatrice wasn't above bribing the fellow either; although he likely wouldn't wait three years for his payment and he might run to Uncle Cedric and confess all.

A mischievous smile twitched the corners of her mouth.

No, she'd have to manage to ruin the gown to delay today's sitting. Next, perhaps, she'd take a tumble and bruise her cheek or develop a week-long megrim.

In truth, the options were endless.

Delightfully endless.

Food poisoning. A skin rash. Sunburn. A summer cold. Weepy eyes. Spilling tea on the painting. Nala knocking the painting over.

Cork powder in Beatrice's eyes would surely irritate them and make them red.

A blackened eye—Beatrice was clumsy after all.

Another ruined gown...

On and on and on.

She would come up with scheme after scheme to prevent her likeness from being painted.

Then what would Uncle do?

With Nala and Teddy trotting at her heels, Beatrice picked her way toward the marble folly in the formal gardens where Uncle had ordered she have her likeness replicated. The satin slippers adorning her feet were better suited for the house's marble and parquet floors, not freshly clipped grass.

Uncle Cedric had seen the gazebo furnished with a floral settee, several throw pillows, flowers, ferns, and other greenery. All in all, the folly was lovely, and had Beatrice not been so put upon, she might have appreciated the effort that had gone into creating the attractive space.

She supposed a garden portrait was a minor concession on his part, as Uncle knew she preferred the outdoors.

More likely, however, was he didn't want her future husband to see the inside of Highbury House. To prevent the money-grubbing potential husband from comprehending Uncle Cedric's wealth and perhaps demanding a dowry, in addition to getting his greedy hands on her twenty thousand pounds.

Uncle Cedric, the heartless wretch, had refused her request to allow Nala and Teddy in the portrait. And that had caused another concern to raise its warty little head...

What if he threatened to take her beloved pets from her if she didn't comply?

Beatrice feared it wasn't beyond him.

Well then, she would have to make certain the series of *mishaps* were wholly believable.

As she tiptoed across the greens, trying not to slip on the grass, she contemplated the precise moment she would trip on the gown and take a fortuitous tumble. She needed to ensure the gown was beyond repair—torn and stained. A couple of rolls across the verdant lawn ought to assure just that.

A tall, dark-haired gentleman attired in gray, stood with his broad back to her.

Odd, she'd expected a shrunken, balding, grizzly-eyebrowed eccentric with hair poking from his ears. Her rather too acute observation of this man revealed he was young and fit.

He'd arranged his painting materials outside the folly on a table.

What had Uncle Cedric said his name was?

Cassius Westbrook?

Uncle boasted the artist was quite accomplished, but Beatrice had never heard of him. That meant little, however, since she knew few people beyond those that she attended Sunday services with and her two friends, Esme and Charlotte.

Nala gave an excited *woof* and dashed forward.

The artist spun around, his dark blue eyes widening upon seeing a ten-stone boarhound descending upon him with the exuberance of a bull detecting a cow in heat.

Lord, he was breathtakingly handsome.

If Beatrice wasn't worried her dog was about to assault him, she might've taken a moment to appreciate his male perfection.

A first for her.

"Nala. Stop!"

When Nala ignored her command, Beatrice hoisted her skirts higher and broke into a run.

Teddy yipped in excitement and tore after Nala.

"Teddy. Nala. Stop this instant!"

Rather than show alarm at having two dogs charging toward him, the handsome artist appeared amused.

He must be familiar with dogs.

Nala never behaved like this and concern for the artist's safety drove Beatrice to lengthen her stride into a sprint. The emeralds at her neck bounced up and down, and one curl plopped onto her shoulder and then another curl. And another.

Nala skidded to a stop in front of Mr. Westbrook, and then, to Beatrice's utter astonishment, rose on her hind legs, placed both her immense paws on his shoulders, and gave him a slobbery doggy kiss before they both toppled to the ground.

"*Oomph.*" Mr. Westbrook landed with a thud, Nala atop him and continuing to lick his face.

Teddy joined the fray, running in circles around the two of them, barking.

"Oh, no." In her shock, Beatrice released her gown, which promptly tangled about her legs.

Rip.

Before she could cry out, she fell, rolling over and landing a few feet from Mr. Westbrook.

She only spared half a second to consider her coiffure and gown's complete destruction. Had she planned this debacle, the outcome couldn't have been better.

"I say, Miss Fairfax. Are you all right?"

Though his tone was gentle, distinct humor underscored Mr. Westbrook's query.

Face scorching with humiliation, Beatrice dared to open her eyes, her gaze colliding with midnight blue. A tremor swept through her.

More than all right, thank you.

He patted Nala's withers as if it were a common occurrence to be knocked on one's back by a huge hound and to have the beast perch upon one's prone form.

Oh, he is quite the loveliest man I've ever seen.

Beatrice offered a shy smile.

"I b-believe, Mr. Westbrook, 'tis I who ought t-to be asking you that question." As she sat up, she slid her attention to Nala. "Nala, off M-Mr. Westbrook. Sit."

Naturally, her blasted stutter would have to manifest.

Nala promptly complied, her tail thumping a happy rhythm.

Tongue lolling, Teddy plopped his little bottom beside her.

Nala never took to strangers.

Never.

"What the devil goes on here?"

FIVE

Highbury House's immaculate lawns

A FEW EMBARRASSING SECONDS LATER

His timing impeccable, Uncle Cedric had arrived.

Beatrice and Mr. Westbrook glanced toward the earl, storming across the lawns.

Clydes, the butler, and Millborn, Beatrice's companion and ladies' maid, trotted in his wake, their faces a mixture of astonishment, apprehension, and concern.

Mr. Westbrook offered Beatrice a genial smile and a wink. "Fear not."

How could he have known her apprehension?

Her heart turned over, and she couldn't prevent her answering smile and slight nod before her common sense returned. She shoved her gown down, noting with carefully hidden satisfaction the torn fabric and grass stains.

In a moment, Uncle Cedric towered above them, infuriated and fairly frothing in frustration.

Uncle did not attempt to help her up.

In a lithe movement, Mr. Westbrook rose to his feet and extended his hand to assist Beatrice.

She slipped her fingers into his wide palm, noting a hint of blue paint beneath one neatly trimmed nail.

"There's been a slight mishap, my lord." Mr. Westbrook didn't appear the least intimidated by Uncle Cedric. He brushed blades of grass from his elbows.

Dark green stained his trousers and jacket, and she hid a wince.

Artists were notoriously poor, and no doubt this was the only decent suit he owned.

Naturally, she'd pay to have his garments cleaned, or if that wasn't possible, replaced.

She bit the inside of her cheek.

How much would that cost?

Her monthly allowance wasn't generous by any means.

"You m-must permit me to pay t-to have your clothing c-cleaned or replaced." Beatrice refused to look in her uncle's direction.

She would find the funds somehow.

"Nothing of the sort." A smile hovering around the edges of his nicely molded mouth, Mr. Westbrook shook his dark head. "A good brushing and all should be well."

He was a rotten liar.

No brushing would remove those embedded smudges.

Scrutinizing her gown, his expression turned rueful. "I fear you are much worse for wear than I, Miss Fairfax."

"Oh, your lovely gown, Miss." Millborn frowned and *tisked* as she took in the ripped, grass-stained fabric. "'Tis beyond repair, I fear."

Hands planted on his hips and eyes narrowed in suspicion, Uncle Cedric's face grew tauter still. "What bloody well happened?"

Beatrice bit her lip.

If she confessed the truth, she worried about what her uncle would do to Nala. He barely tolerated her dogs' presence as it was.

Nala chose that moment to pad over to Mr. Westbrook and nuzzle his palm.

Giving the dog a good-natured grin, he patted her enormous head.

"Nala's greeting was a trifle more exuberant than either I or Miss Fairfax anticipated, my lord. I'm flattered, in truth."

Beatrice liked Mr. Westbrook all the more for defending her pet.

"That still doesn't explain how you and my niece both came to be rolling around on the ground, Lord Cassius."

Lord Cassius?

Uncle had failed to mention *that* important detail.

And he and Beatrice were hardly rolling around.

Well, she *had* rolled—twice, in fact. The first was from the momentum of her fall and the second was to ensure the gown was good and stained. She'd even pressed her bum, shoulders, and knees into the ground as she turned to insure the latter.

"Your niece feared for my safety and in her haste to reach her pet, she slipped." Lord Cassius gave her feet a pointed look. "Satin slippers upon grass are much as skates upon ice."

As Beatrice had never ice-skated or worn satin slippers outdoors before, she had no way of knowing if that was actually true. And Uncle could only blame himself for directing her to wear the slippers.

Nevertheless, she couldn't regret the unanticipated implementation and success of her scheme, even if she hadn't initiated it.

In succession, Uncle Cedric glowered at her, Nala, the neatly arranged art supplies, Teddy quietly observing the ordeal, and finally at Beatrice once more.

It was quite telling that he didn't direct his ire toward Lord Cassius Westbrook.

"We'll need to reschedule the portrait session, I

suppose," Uncle Cedric conceded with as much enthusiasm as a person facing a tooth pulling or a carbuncle lancing. He gave a brisk shake of his head. "Not outside next time. I don't want another frock destroyed by her clumsiness."

Beatrice was careful to keep her expression benign, but she didn't miss Lord Cassius's raven eyebrow flying high on his forehead at Uncle Cedric's snide remark. A second later, he schooled his expression, but censure flashed in his beautiful blue eyes, the color of the ocean at twilight.

Uncle considered Lord Cassius, a speculative gleam in his cold, gray eyes. "Have you a space in your studio?"

Oh, bother.

She hadn't considered that.

How could she have the dogs ruin the project if they weren't with her?

"I do, or I should say, I can arrange to have." Lord Cassius angled his head, his astute gaze taking in Uncle Cedric. "Wouldn't you rather have Miss Fairfax painted in familiar surroundings?"

Beatrice had the distinct impression he saw beyond her uncle's public façade.

"No, I believe a neutral environment is more suitable. Less chance of another disaster."

Or so he thinks.

Giving another decisive nod, Uncle veered his attention to Millborn. "You'll chaperone Beatrice during the sittings. See that another gown is ordered. I'll pay twice the normal fees if it's finished by next week."

He didn't even trust her to select another gown.

"As you wish, my lord." The elderly servant folded her hands. Millborn didn't dare say anything else. She'd never once crossed Uncle Cedric during the many years she'd been assigned to tend to Beatrice.

He paid her well for her compliance and biddableness, but what was the aged servant to do?

Defy him and get tossed to the curb?

"Not green this time. It makes her look common...like a wood nymph or sprite. She needs to appear sophisticated and noble." Uncle Cedric raked a critical gaze over Beatrice. "Coral or ivory, I think."

"I recommend cornflower blue, my lord." Lord Cassius made the suggestion as confidently as if he addressed a peer.

Perhaps he did.

Only younger sons of dukes and marquesses bore the honorific lord before their given name.

Just who was Lord Cassius Westbrook?

Giving him a sharp look, Uncle Cedric considered the suggestion. "Why?"

"That shade will pair well with her coloring, brightening her eyes, softening her freckles, and complementing her hair." He sent Beatrice a reassuring glance. "Besides, you specified she appear noble. Blue has long been associ-ated with regalness and royalty."

"I *c-can* hear y-you, you kn-know." Beatrice didn't know where she summoned the gumption to be so bold, but no one enjoyed being discussed like they weren't there or were a commodity to present to buyers.

"I'd hold my tongue, gel." Uncle Cedric speared her with a wrath-filled glower before directing his attention back to Lord Cassius. "You're the artist. I'd dress her in chartreuse if you thought it would make her more attractive."

Heat scoured Beatrice's cheeks as she signaled Nala to come to her side. The hound complied instantly. Teddy trotted over and, with his chocolate brown eyes, silently begged her to pick him up. She did at once, to hide the distress her uncle's unkindness caused her in front of a stranger.

"You mistake me." A steeliness entered Lord Cassius's tenor. "I never implied Miss Fairfax needed enhancement. For I assure you, the canvas shall adore her, should she choose to wear wren brown or mourning gray. I also suggest no jewelry or cosmetics and that she wear her hair down."

Beatrice hid a pleased smile in Teddy's shoulder.

No one had ever championed her before, nor compli-mented her appearance.

"*Hmph.*" Uncle grunted his doubt. "I don't want her

to look like the Virgin Mary, Westbrook—not that she could with *that* hair.”

He flicked his hand disparagingly toward her head.

“I assure you, my lord, the likeness shall be acceptable to your strict standards.” Again, a less than deferential tone infused Lord Cassius's flinty response.

“Next week, Friday?” Uncle clasped his hands behind his back, a hint of irritation hardening his jaw. “Same time?”

“No. Morning.” Lord Cassius collected his paintbrushes and as he wrapped them in a linen cloth, shook his head. “The lighting is much better. More flattering. Besides, my studio can get quite warm in the afternoon.”

Lord Cassius glanced at Beatrice. “Ten?”

He asked her. Not Uncle, but *her.*

“Yes.” She dared a nod and refused to look in her uncle's direction, certain she'd find nothing but contempt etched upon his features. At least she hadn't stuttered when she answered.

“Get yourself into the house and clean up, Beatrice.” Uncle Cedric raised an eyebrow. “You look like common riffraff. Millborn, return the emeralds to my study.”

“Yes, my lord,” Millborn said in her usual subservient manner.

Beatrice half-turned to go, but Lord Cassius hailed her.

“Miss Fairfax?”

"Yes, Lord Cassius?"

He swept his mouth upward into a charming grin. "We were not properly introduced."

She darted a glance toward Uncle Cedric, who had the good grace to flush to his hairline.

No doubt he hadn't considered her worthy of an introduction.

"I am Lord Cassius Westbrook, youngest son of the Duke of Latham."

That answered that question.

He flashed a grin, so startling in its beauty, Beatrice couldn't help but blink. Her heart forgot to beat for an instant, and her breath hung suspended. Surely the earth ceased rotating as well.

"Well, one of his two youngest sons," he said. "I have a twin."

Good Lord.

There were *two* of them?

She dipped into a curtsy, quite pleased she didn't wobble in the least. "I-I look forward t-to our next meeting, sir."

"As do I." He grinned again, and she could almost believe he meant it.

Beatrice had barely stuttered while speaking to him.

Her heart sang all the way back to the house, which was just silly because she still meant to sabotage Lord

Cassius Westbrook's painting. Even if he was the most alluring figure of masculinity that she'd ever set eyes upon.

SIX

Sussex Square-Kempton
Brighton, England

ONE WEEK LATER ~ A COUPLE OF MINUTES TO TEN IN THE MORNING

Cassius adjusted a cushion on the used royal blue velvet Gillow armchair he'd purchased that week, along with a cast-off Aubusson carpet, a tapestry, draperies, and a marble-top half table. Items he'd sell as soon as he completed Beatrice Fairfax's portrait—in about six weeks, if all went well.

Head tilted, he adjusted the chair's angle a few inches to ensure the natural light would complement her.

That is better.

In truth, he itched to paint Miss Fairfax...to see if he could recreate the ribbons of gold, copper, bronze, and sienna in her hair. To dapple her ivory skin with those precocious freckles. Then there was that adorable dimple in her chin that he longed to put to canvas.

He'd considered writing to his parents to request they send similar items from Hefferwickshire House, the ducal country estate in Cumberland, but the furnishings would likely not have arrived in time for today's sitting. Besides, he didn't want his parents speculating about the urgent request for elegant decor.

They worried enough about him.

Barely a week ago, he'd received a letter from Mother and Father.

Mother missed him—she'd seen him but two months ago.

A visit was in order soon, Father had declared. Cassius expected the duke and duchess to present themselves in Brighton within the next fortnight.

Both prayed all was well, which Cassius interpreted to mean they fretted he might need financial assistance but was too proud to ask.

Yes, he was proud but also determined. Of all his siblings, at almost eight and twenty, he alone had yet to establish himself. Actually, that wasn't entirely accurate. After two decades, his eldest half-brother Layton had left

His Majesty's Army and had yet to decide what to do with the rest of his life.

Honestly, Cassius had believed Layton would die, an army officer. This change of plans took the family by surprise, but as always, the Westbrooks rallied around their kin, offering support and encouragement.

This past week, Cassius had neglected his seascape painting, directing all his attention toward creating a pleasant setting for Miss Fairfax's portrait sitting. Foolish by far, since he hadn't time to spare if he meant to finish the required paintings for the exhibition.

Still, he wasn't overly concerned.

He would manage.

Hands on his hips, he surveyed his workmanship.

Would she like the scene he'd staged?

Why he should care what a woman thought he'd met but once for less than thirty minutes, Cassius could not fathom. Had he an ounce of sense, he would have refused Lord Highbury's request to paint her in his studio. He had never done so before, preferring to reserve his workspace for private use.

He had no intention of doing so again.

Regardless, something about Beatrice Fairfax beckoned to him. Her expressive hazel-green gaze assessed him with a refreshing openness and lack of artifice. At her uncle's caustic rebuke the other day, pink had blossomed across her heart-shaped face.

Highbury's callousness toward her rankled Cassius.

The earl treated her like a nuisance—a smelly beggar or a pesky, stray dog.

Cassius cast a glance at the picture window at the front of his studio as a gleaming burgundy coach rumbled to a stop before his establishment.

Right on time.

His pulse skipped in anticipation, but he quickly subdued his excitement.

This was a job.

Nothing more.

There was no room in his life for a romantic interest in any female. Constanza had successfully rendered his heart as cold as stone. It was simply the anticipation of creating a miniature, he repeated to himself for the hundredth time.

It took particular skill to paint a miniature, and he welcomed the challenge.

Arranging his features into a neutral expression, he exited the front entrance just as the coachman swung the carriage door open.

Wearing a light ivory cloak with the hood pulled up over her head, Miss Fairfax appeared in the opening. She offered him a shy smile as the coachman lowered the step.

Coming to his senses, Cassius approached the vehicle and offered her a hand down. "No dogs today?"

She placed her gloved hand in his and alit from the

conveyance, nimble as the wood sprite her uncle had compared her to last week. "I wasn't sure if y-you would welcome them in your s-studio."

"I can see no harm. I like dogs. We have Dalmatians at Hefferwickshire House—my family home. In truth, I'd like to include them in the portrait. Teddy in your lap and Nala lying beside the chair."

"Uncle doesn't want them in the painting." Disappointed resignation darkened her eyes to the shade of the ocean before a pending gale.

"Ah, but he said he would agree to whatever I suggested, did he not?" That was a stretch, but Highbury wouldn't likely appreciate the delay starting the portrait process over would entail if he remained adamant about no pets in the painting. Cassius could see how much her beloved dogs meant to Beatrice, and they should be immortalized with her.

Miss Fairfax gifted him a brilliant smile. "I shall bring them next time."

Millborn poked her head out, and after glancing up and down the lane, permitted Cassius to assist her from the coach as well.

"Welcome to my humble studio, ladies."

Miss Fairfax granted him another cheerful smile, but her chaperone merely inclined her graying head. She plainly did not want to attend Miss Fairfax for the sittings.

"When should Hampton return, Lord Cassius?" Millborn asked.

Hampton must be the coachman.

"Four hours." Cassius should have a rough sketch completed by then.

"I'll be back to fetch you at two, then." Hampton touched his hat and, after climbing onto the driver's seat and calling, "Walk on," flicked the reins.

The matched grays dutifully moved forward, their hooves *clip-clopping* pleasantly on the cobbles.

"Shall we?" Cassius extended an arm toward his studio.

Millborn entered first, surveying every inch of the interior with admirable diligence.

Miss Fairfax followed, her eyes round with pleasure.

"Oh, I've n-never been inside an artist's studio before." She grinned up at him, excitement sparkling in her eyes as she pulled the ivory silk cloak from her head. That curtain of sunrise-colored curls swung loosely about her shoulders, down her back, and just skimmed the top of her derriere.

When she untied the ribbon at her throat and let the cloak slip from her shoulders, Cassius nearly gasped aloud and was hard put not to stare.

Breathtaking.

Her uncle was wrong.

Bloody sodding wrong.

Beatrice Fairfax was an incomparable.

Not an English rose, to be sure. No, this vibrant beauty was a canna lily, striking and elegant.

What a delight putting her features on canvas would be.

If only Cassius were painting a full-sized portrait.

Why can't I?

SEVEN

Indeed, he could switch the painting with one of the other pieces in the exhibition.

The tones of her luxurious hair mirrored her lively spirit and warmth, and her infectious smile was a beacon of light. In short, Beatrice Fairfax was a masterpiece of nature.

How could her uncle be so blind to her loveliness?

By God, people would stop in their tracks to gaze upon her likeness.

Cassius forced his focus back to the moment. "Would you like a brief tour of the studio?"

"Oh, yes, please." She laid her cloak over a nearby chair. "If it w-wouldn't be an inconvenience."

"*Ahem.*" Millborn cleared her throat, not quite in disapproval, but certainly in deterrence. "Shouldn't you begin at once?"

"Forgive me, Millborn." Cassius flashed her his most disarming smile, and the woman's starchy demeanor promptly transformed into doe-eyed adoration.

It was terrible of him to manipulate the servant, but Cassius wanted to share his work and studio with Beatrice. The desire made absolutely no sense, but he refused to analyze his motives or the impetus prompting him.

"I know sittings can be quite tedious. I hope you'll indulge me, for I presumed to prepare a cozy area for you." Cassius indicated a corner beside another window with an overstuffed armchair, a table with a tea service and steaming pot of tea, an assortment of biscuits he'd purchased from the baker three blocks away, and two gossip rags.

The maid's eyes lit up like fireworks over Vauxhall Gardens.

"How thoughtful of you, Lord Cassius," she fairly purred.

"Millborn, why d-don't you make yourself comfortable while Lord Cassius g-gives me a short tour?" Miss Fairfax touched the maid's shoulder in affection. "I kn-know your arthritis has been acting up."

Most nobles had no idea when their domestics ailed. It

said much about Miss Fairfax that she not only noticed but also cared.

Indecision flickered across the aged servant's face as she glanced covetously at the tempting array a few feet away. "If you're quite certain..."

"Indeed." Miss Fairfax—Beatrice—glanced up at Cassius.

Surely it could do no harm for him to think of her by her given name.

Did she know Beatrice meant bringer of joy?

"My studio is not overly large, as you can see, Millborn. Do make yourself comfortable." He offered her his arm and her eyes went round as twin moons. "I promise, you shall be able to see us at all times."

Millborn darted Beatrice an astonished glance before breaking into a toothy grin, and laying her hand upon his forearm, allowed Cassius to escort her to her little nook.

"You are most thoughtful, Lord Cassius." Once settled comfortably, she shooed them away. "Go on with you. We cannot dally too long. His lordship wants the portrait finished right quick."

Millborn sent Beatrice an apologetic glance. "Oh, dear, I didn't mean..."

"I know, Millborn." Despite her reassuring words and accompanying smile, the corners of Beatrice's eyes tightened, as did her rosebud mouth.

What woman was eager to have her likeness painted,

knowing it would be used to find her a husband not of her choosing?

Honestly, Cassius was of a mind to take his time in completing the project—particularly as he would also secretly be creating a full-sized painting. Not just to spite the pretentious ponce, but to delay Beatrice's unpleasant fate as long as possible.

He couldn't help but notice her stutter wasn't as apparent when her uncle wasn't around. Likely, the over-bearing, unfeeling cur agitated the condition.

"Come, let me show you my current work." Cassius sought to distract Beatrice from the dark thoughts that no doubt paraded through her mind. "It's a seascape."

She nodded and stepped away, murmuring beneath her breath, "I'll wager she's asleep w-within fifteen minutes."

All the better, for he intended to converse with Beatrice while he worked. She stirred his curiosity, and the more he knew about his patrons, the more authentic replicas of their likenesses he could create.

He discovered from asking around Brighton—discreetly, of course—that Beatrice had been in the earl's care since a toddler and there was a scandal surrounding her birth. Her mother had run off with an Italian lace merchant only to return less than three years later, ill, unwed, and with a small child in tow. Seraphina Fairfax had died within a month of arriving in Brighton.

Society didn't treat those born on the wrong side of the blanket kindly, and clearly, Lord Highbury resented his niece, rather than cherishing her.

Cassius glanced over his shoulder.

With a ginger biscuit in one hand and tendrils of steam spiraling upward from the cup of tea before her, Millborn picked up a gossip rag. She would be content for some time.

"Tell me about yourself, Miss Fairfax."

Propriety forbid him from addressing her by her given name—*yet*.

He steered Beatrice toward the seascape, covered with a cloth. "Have you any hobbies? Likes? Interests? Do you draw or paint?"

Shaking her head, she gave a little self-deprecating laugh.

"I confess my drawing skills are d-dismal at best, Lord Cassius. The only ability I possess is a knack for caring for injured animals. I rescued Nala and Teddy. I also have other pets who were too injured to return to the wild."

Her kindness and tender heartedness didn't surprise Cassius. She possessed a gentle spirit.

He'd sensed it from the beginning, for he did too. Of all the eight Westbrook siblings, he was the most sensitive.

"I also want to travel someday." A faraway look entered her eyes. "To warm, exotic places."

Like Italy?

Despite Constanza's betrayal, he still loved the Mediterranean country.

After uncovering the seascape, he stood back, arms folded. "What do you think?"

Normally, he didn't let anyone see his work before completion.

"May I?" She flicked her hand toward the canvas resting on the easel.

"Of course."

Beatrice approached the painting. A finger on her dimpled chin and head tilted, she studied the artwork. "I feel the storm's power."

She slid him a sideways glance, and he gave her an encouraging nod.

"Go on," he said.

"I see wrath and fury, but also a wild, uncontrolled beauty." She hadn't stuttered at all.

Did tension and anxiety bring about the disability?

"The light isn't quite right."

Why had Cassius told her that?

"Really?" Forehead puckered, she returned her attention to the painting. "I think it's stunning. It feels alive. I can almost hear the waves crashing on the shore, the rain p-pelting the rocks, the wind howling, and even smell the ocean's salty tang."

Suddenly feeling foolish, he grunted.

"We should get started." His abrupt change in tone

caused a flicker of uncertainty in Beatrice's eyes and a pinch of guilt too. "We can finish the tour another day."

"Certainly." She approached the blue velvet chair and, after sending her chaperone a swift glance, lowered her voice. "I t-think it only fair to t-tell you that I am an unwilling p-participant in this venture."

Ah, yes.

Upset definitely aggravated her speech impediment.

"I surmised as much." A half-smile tugged Cassius's mouth upward. He appreciated her candor. "So why did you agree to sit for the portrait?"

With inherent grace, she sank onto the seat.

Why did her uncle think her clumsy?

"Uncle Cedric threatened t-to toss me out onto the s-street if I d-didn't."

Cassius inhaled long breath to prevent the foul oath, tapping at the back of his teeth, from exploding from his mouth.

Cedric Fairfax, Earl of Highbury, was an unconscionable, sodding rotter.

Cassius took his time buttoning his smock so his temper might ebb before approaching her.

Mindful to keep his tone low so Millborn couldn't overhear and report back to the earl, he asked, "And you've nowhere to go or anyone to take you in?"

He knew that she didn't. The townsfolk spoke of her kindly but with pity too.

Beatrice shook her head. "Nowhere and no one."

Her fragile smile nearly shattered his heart.

"Don't look so distraught, Lord Cassius. I c-come into a twenty-thousand-pound inheritance from my maternal grandmother when I turn five and twenty. I j-just have to figure out how to avoid matrimony for another two and a half years."

So that made her two and twenty.

He had thought her older. She possessed the maturity and comportment of someone who had seen a few more years.

"Most young women are eager to marry." He pointed to the chair's armrest. "Place your right arm on the chair, and your left hand in your lap."

She complied, her movements naturally agile.

"*Most* young women don't have a mother betrayed by her Italian lover."

Italian?

Cassius jerked his head up.

"Mama didn't know he was married until they were in Italy." She shrugged. "By then, she carried me."

Another perfidious Italian.

What were the chances of that?

Not that Italians were any more inclined to treachery than any other people. Goodness and evil didn't play favorites.

"As such, I'm not altogether keen on marrying." She

ran her slender fingers across the blue silk covering her thighs.

Beatrice meant it. How unusual.

"I would much prefer to control the rudder that navigates my life and not be dependent on another who may or may not have my best interests at heart," she said, no hint of regret or apology in her tone or expression.

"I was betrothed once." He hadn't intended to reveal that detail.

"Oh?" Surprise whisked across her face.

Cassius met her intrigued gaze.

Stop, embecile. She doesn't need to know your sordid, romantic past.

And yet, the words spilled forth, acrid and icy, despite his mental chastisement. "She tossed me aside for a richer, more important fellow."

Compassion softened Beatrice's features. "That must have been awful for you."

"*She* was also Italian."

EIGHT

Still Sussex Square-Kempton

A QUARTER OF TWO THAT SAME DAY

Beatrice permitted herself to study Cassius Westbrook as he worked. Midnight brows drawn together in concentration, he glanced up every few minutes, skimming that riveting gaze over her like a cobalt caress, before focusing intently on the easel once more.

It shouldn't surprise her he had once been betrothed.

A man possessing his good looks was bound to attract women like ants to honey. From the arctic coolness that had washed over his features and frozen his tone, he'd not forgiven his former betrothed for her betrayal.

He must've loved the woman desperately.

Sympathy engulfed Beatrice for his suffering, though why she should feel empathy for a man she scarcely knew baffled her. She supposed her ability to care for animals in distress had extended to him. A natural reaction toward any suffering creature, to be sure.

Still, she couldn't help wondering what that kind of all-consuming love felt like. To give it and to receive it? Having lacked being loved most of her life, she had nothing to compare the powerful sentiment to.

That Cassius yet suffered for giving his heart to an unworthy wretch, only reaffirmed Beatrice's determination not to yield to such imprudence. She would direct her affections to her pets and receive unconditional love in return.

No man would ever have the opportunity to betray her as her father had Mama.

"Did you s-study art in Italy?"

Drat her unquenchable curiosity and her stutter.

Lord Cassius must've been in Italy to study and train. Even Beatrice understood how unusual that was for a duke's son.

He paused in *scritching* the pencil across the canvas for a half-second before shrugging. "I did. For several years."

"But you left after your broken betrothal?" Her dashed tongue refused to be muzzled, but at least she'd managed a sentence without stuttering.

"I was summoned home by my grandmother. But I had decided it was time to leave in any event." He kicked his mouth upward on one side, giving him a boyish appearance that in no way diminished his roguish good looks. "One does not dismiss a summons from Grandmama, particularly at Christmastide, and especially when she hints at dire circumstances."

Beatrice had never known her grandparents.

"I'm sorry." And she was.

However, having never loved anyone romantically, she couldn't fathom the depths of his pain. But neither had she suffered a broken wing, a brutal beating, starvation, or her leg caught in a snare, but that didn't prevent her from sympathizing with her pets.

A shuttered expression came over Lord Cassius's features, and he returned to his work.

Clearly, he didn't want to talk about his former betrothed.

It was none of Beatrice's business in any event, and she ought not to have probed. Resigned to her curiosity remaining unsatiated, she continued her silent assessment of the man who'd intrigued her this past week.

She permitted herself the luxury of examining him at her leisure.

He certainly pleased the eye.

He ought to have *his* likeness painted.

Today he wore unremarkable black trousers tucked

into well-worn boots. He'd removed his dusky blue jacket before donning his paint-smattered smock, giving her a glimpse of finely molded shoulders, chest, and back. His simply knotted neckcloth and blue and black striped waistcoat suggested quality but not ostentatiousness.

"Are you an identical twin?"

There went her thoughts again, making their way to her tongue and out into the air without a by-your-leave.

He gave a brief nod.

"Darius and I used to swap places, and even our parents were none the wiser."

Glancing over the easel, he met her gaze and a tiny little current of something thrilling zipped along her veins.

"Did you miss not having siblings, Miss Fairfax?"

His question jerked Beatrice's attention from his long-lean legs to his contoured face.

He'd kept up a constant litany as he worked, which rather surprised her. She would have thought an artist needed silence to complete his best work.

"I didn't know anything else." In point of fact, Beatrice had been horribly lonely. The servants were kind, but except for Millborn who was assigned to watch her, they had other tasks to see to.

"What about you, Lord Cassius? Have you other brothers or sisters b-besides your twin?"

He chuckled, a pleasant and resonating rumble in his broad chest.

Uncle Cedric expressed humor so seldom—and when he did, it was usually snide and at her expense—she found herself mesmerized by the simple sound.

For surely that was what caused her deepening interest in Cassius Westbrook—how very different he was from her dour uncle.

What else could it be?

"Indeed, I do." Affection creased the outer corners of his eyes. "*Five* older brothers and one younger sister. Two of my older brothers are half-brothers, and my sister is unlike any other woman you've ever met." He met her gaze, a twinkle in his. "I think you'd like her. She also loves dogs, and shoots and rides better than most men."

"How wonderful." Beatrice twitched her nose back and forth.

"Is there a reason you're imitating a rabbit, Miss Fairfax?"

Again, an undercurrent of humor belied his somber expression.

"Might I scratch my nose?"

"Of course." Grinning, Lord Cassius nodded and circled the pencil in the air. "I'm not an ogre. If you need to get up and stretch, get a drink, scratch your nose, or have a bite to eat, just let me know. I'd prefer a contented subject. Any discomfort will manifest in your bearing and features."

Beatrice longed to stretch her muscles, use the necessary, and a bite to eat would be welcome too. She'd remember to bring a snack next time. Nonetheless, something held her in place.

No, not *something*.

Someone.

Him.

Prior to this, no man had caught her attention, let alone one that looked as if he'd stepped straight from heaven. Normally, she didn't indulge in girlish musings and infatuations.

But then, she'd never met the likes of Lord Cassius Westbrook.

It wasn't just his stunning masculine good looks, either.

She liked *him*.

Yes, he was serious, perhaps some might call him solemn, but humor frequently shone in his eyes and quirked his mouth. But it was his kindness and gentleness that beckoned her. She thought he might be as nice as he appeared—a rare and unusual quality amongst the peerage.

Even younger sons of nobles, particularly privileged dukes' sons, believed themselves above everyone else. No one could measure up to their inflated opinions of themselves.

She'd witnessed that first-hand with Uncle Cedric.

Lord, the man was a pompous arse.

Beatrice hadn't detected a hint of snobbery about Lord Cassius, not even when he'd introduced himself as the Duke of Latham's son. She hadn't heard of the duke, but then again, she didn't travel in fashionable circles— not even in this resort township favored by aristocrats.

It brought her pleasure to observe Lord Cassius, and sitting still these past hours gave her ample opportunity. Soon enough, she'd have a chance to cause an *accidental* mishap.

A stab of guilt speared her.

She almost felt remorse for her plan to destroy his work. *Almost.* However, self-preservation allowed her to push her guilt into a corner of her mind and slam the door on any regret.

She skimmed her attention over the other paintings on display.

Uncle had been correct.

Though she was no expert, even she could see that Cassius Westbrook possessed talent—exceptional talent.

In her cozy corner, Millborn softly snored, having fallen asleep as Beatrice had predicted, but only after consuming every single biscuit. Uncle rarely permitted Cook to bake sweet treats, claiming they would ruin his figure.

He fussed more over his appearance than any woman Beatrice had ever met. She vowed he plucked his eyebrows too.

"I think we are done for today." Cassius took one last glance at the easel and set the pencil aside.

As if on cue, Millborn snorted and startled herself awake. She yawned and blinked. "Did I hear you say we are finished for today, Lord Cassius?"

Nodding, he spared a quick glance to her corner. "We are."

Millborn stood, her movements stiff and slow.

She really ought to retire, but she had no family either. Uncle Cedric—the inconsiderate miser—had never mentioned pensioning the elderly woman. Therefore, necessity compelled her to continue to work.

Another reason Beatrice must have control over her inheritance. She could set Millborn up in a cozy cottage with a monthly stipend. Or even allow the dear to travel with her if she so wished. Since Mama's death—from a broken heart and shame, Beatrice was convinced—

Millborn had been the closest thing to a mother Beatrice had known.

Beatrice unfolded from the chair, almost grimacing as her muscles objected to the movement. She gave the back of the easel a pointed look. "May I see?"

"No." Lord Cassius gave her a sideways smile, even as he draped a cloth over the easel. "You may not. I never permit a patron to see my work in progress."

There was a finality to his answer, and she didn't press him.

As he unbuttoned his paint-stained smock, he crossed the room. After he'd hung it on a hook and shrugged into his jacket, he faced her. "I should like you to return in three days for another four hours."

"As you wish." Beatrice collected her silk cloak. "Are you certain I should bring Nala and Teddy?"

If Uncle Cedric hadn't directed Millborn to chaperone her, Beatrice could simply walk to the studio with her dogs. That wouldn't raise suspicion, for she walked about Brighton all the time with her pets. She would have simply worn a morning gown and changed when she arrived for the sitting.

After sliding the cloak over her pretty new blue gown, she tied the ribbon at her throat.

"Yes, bring them." Lord Cassius nodded. "You have a different demeanor about you with your pets nearby. I'd like to capture that in your likeness. Once your uncle sees the portrait, he'll understand.

"The master won't like it," Millborn said, crossing to them, unable to hide a slight limp, no doubt caused by stiff knee or hip joints. "Not a bit."

"Leave the matter to me." Unlike most people who encountered Uncle Cedric, the earl did not intimidate Lord Cassius. "I shall take full responsibility."

Once again, his confidence impressed Beatrice.

It probably infuriated Uncle.

In truth, it wasn't just Lord Cassius's confidence or

self-assurance that raised him in her estimation. Uncle Cedric was confident to the point of arrogance and mulishness. No, it was Lord Cassius's fearlessness combined with diplomacy and compassion.

Uncle lacked the latter qualities.

Beatrice didn't try to dissuade Lord Cassius from including Nala and Teddy in her portrait. The worst that could happen was Uncle would demand a second go at the painting.

If not rendered by Lord Cassius, then by another artist. And that would take time. Not two and a half years, but she welcomed anything that delayed the painting's completion and subsequently, forcing her to trudge down the aisle against her will.

Not that she intended to let the painting progress to the point of Uncle Cedric ever seeing the finished product. How fortuitous that Lord Cassius wanted her to bring her pets to his studio. All manner of *accidents* might occur.

Hadn't dear Nala already proven that?

Beatrice raised her gaze to Lord Cassius, startled to find him observing her intently. He saw much more than he commented upon. She understood the power of observation, for she practiced it too. It was, however, rather uncanny to be the object and not the observer.

"Two pence for your thoughts, Miss Fairfax."

Chagrin almost made her drop her gaze, but avoidance would certainly give her away.

She managed what she hoped was a winsome smile rather than a guilt-ridden one. "I assure you, they are not worth t-two farthings."

"Why is it I doubt that?" He cast a side-long glance toward the easel. "I think you've forgotten I'm an artist. We can see what most people try to hide." He pointed to his eyes—so striking, so blue. "The eyes speak—windows to the soul and all that."

"Quoting Shakespeare?" She didn't much care for the famous bard's works. A fact she kept to herself since so many revered the playwright.

Lord Cassius shook his head, a dark shock of hair falling over his high forehead. "Actually, I referred to the Roman philosopher Cicero, when he said, 'The face is a picture of the mind as the eyes are its interpreter.'"

"So you think you can read my mind?" He couldn't possibly know her thoughts—her devious scheme.

He cocked an aristocratic eyebrow.

"You, Miss Fairfax, are far more complex than you let on."

Beatrice cast a worried glance at Millborn, who had perked up at the conversation's strange turn.

"I have n-no idea what you mean, Lord C-Cassius. I am simply and dutifully sitting for a portrait."

Beatrice purposefully widened her eyes to appear

innocent, except her blasted stutter gave her away. Up to now, she'd barely stuttered in his presence today.

Eyebrows pinched together, Millborn wavered her attention between them, obviously confused and suspicious. "Did something happen while I napped?"

The coach rolled to a stop in front of the studio, saving Beatrice from having to answer. Instead, she took Millborn's elbow.

"We'll see you Friday, Lord Cassius."

"Don't forget the dogs," he reminded with a good-natured smile.

Was he teasing her?

Once settled inside the coach, Beatrice leaned forward and peered out the window.

Lord Cassius stood in the doorway, a bemused smile bending his mouth.

On a naughty impulse, she stuck her tongue out, and he threw his head back and laughed.

As she settled back into the seat, her blood rushing through her veins, the truth hit Beatrice with such force that she slumped against the seat.

That was what flirting felt like.

And she liked it.

Liked it very much, indeed.

NINE

Brighton Seafront-Promenade

TWO DAYS LATER ~ MIDMORNING

Cassius scooped up a handful of pebbles and, contemplating the play of the ocean's waves along the shoreline, began tossing them one at a time into the foamy waters. A brisk breeze teased the sea, creating small white peaks and ruffling his hair.

Several gulls, carried by the wind's currents, floated gracefully over the pristine greenish-blue water, sunlight glittering like a million diamonds on the choppy surface.

Frustrated at his inability to still get the lighting exactly right on his storm seascape painting, he'd put aside his brushes and decided a brisk walk and fresh air along the shore might inspire him.

Only bothering to slip on a hunting jacket, he'd grabbed an apple to eat on the way and walked straight from his studio to the beach. He tossed another smooth black pebble into the gently rolling waves, followed by an equally smooth gray stone.

While perfection eluded his seascape, he was quite pleased with how Beatrice Fairfax's portraits were coming along. Without consent from either her or Lord Highbury, Cassius had elected to secretly create a full-sized portrait as he'd contemplated doing the other day.

He suspected there'd be hell to pay if Highbury found out, and he bloody well did not know what he'd do with the portrait after the art exhibition.

Regardless, it was an injustice to confine Beatrice's unique beauty to a tiny, three-inch miniature. She deserved to be displayed in all her rare glory, even if it was only at the show in London.

He hadn't decided if he'd allow Beatrice to see the full-sized portrait.

It was her right, of course.

But Cassius felt certain she would object. He'd glimpsed the swiftly hidden mutiny in her glance the other day. She wasn't as amendable to having her likeness replicated as she affected. Her reticence was caused by more than the duress and coercion from her uncle too, but

Cassius couldn't identify what her reluctance stemmed from, besides the obvious.

She didn't want an arranged marriage.

He knew full well he overstepped the bounds with this clandestine project, but as he wasn't charging a fee to paint the portrait and he was still in need of paintings for the British Institution, he justified his actions.

Cassius Nathan Everett Westbrook, that's a bloody stretch and you deuced well know it.

Curving his mouth into a self-deprecatory smile, he pitched the rest of the pebbles into the sea.

Aye, no small amount of truth there.

Woof.

Woof. Woof.

Half-turning toward the barking dog, he spied Beatrice Fairfax walking toward him, her ever-faithful canine companions at her side. Her eyes widened the merest bit upon seeing him, and he vowed her cheeks reddened.

Was her flushed face because of their last encounter when she'd stuck her tongue out at him?

She reminded him of his spirited sister, Althelia, but he doubted Beatrice Fairfax had ever dared stick her tongue out at anyone before, not even as a lass. Nay, she seemed the type who did her utmost to obey and remain as invisible as possible.

What a tyrant Highbury must be.

Upon seeing Cassius, Nala fairly danced in excitement, but the lead fastened to the boarhound's collar kept her at her mistress's side.

Cassius set off in their direction.

Woof. Woof.

Nala wagged her tail so hard that her back end wiggled and, given the hound's immense size, that was something to behold.

Not to be outdone, Teddy pranced about.

Yap. Yappity, yap, yap.

"Hush, you two. Lord Cassius sees you." Beatrice's musical tone held no real censure, nor did she stutter. "How could he not when your manners are so poor?"

"Good morning, Miss Fairfax." Cassius pressed a palm to his waist and gave a half bow. "Morning, Nala and Teddy."

Nala and Teddy plopped their haunches on the sand and raised their paws.

Cassius dutifully shook each furry appendage as he swept his appreciative gaze over Beatrice.

She was a breath of fresh air—a lily in a world of roses, and she stood out all the more because of it.

It was the artist in him that admired her originality and nothing else, he reminded himself.

Hadn't he sampled romance once?

Madly and wholeheartedly?

Indeed, he had, and love had left a bitter flavor in his mouth and his soul charred and warped.

Cassius wasn't interested in traipsing down that treacherous path again—particularly with a woman destined for matrimony. Thus, he resolved to remain a bachelor and dedicate his life to his art.

She was his mistress.

He needed no other, nor did he want the complications and vexations that came with loving a flesh and blood woman.

Even one as unique and appealing as Beatrice Fairfax.

Her simple straw bonnet tied with a white ribbon beneath her pert chin matched her unadorned spencer. Simplicity suited her. The skirts of her peach gown billowing behind her, Beatrice laughed.

"Good morning, Lord Cassius." Happiness lit her pretty hazel eyes and the ocean air brought a becoming bloom to her cheeks. "The dogs seldom take to anyone but me, especially men."

"I'm flattered they remember me." Squinting slightly against the bright sun, he asked, "What brings you out on this fine morn?"

He patted each dog on the head, earning him adoring brown-eyed gazes.

A shadow flickered across Beatrice's face, but she swiftly hid it with another bright smile. "I hadn't walked the d-dogs in several d-days."

Her stutter's reappearance gave her distress away. More likely, she needed a reason to leave Highbury House and her uncle's authoritarian overreach.

"And I needed to d-drop my other walking b-boots off at the shoe repair for new soles."

Most nobles discarded shoes before they became worn enough to require repairs.

He eyed her gown and spencer closely.

They were well made, as one would expect from the ward of an earl, but not extravagant or the first stare of fashion as was the Earl of Highbury's attire. Nor were they new. Upon further inspection, Cassius concluded they were at least two—probably three seasons—old.

Was the earl a penny-pinching miser, to boot? Or did he reserve his parsimony for Beatrice alone? Moreover, was Highbury's resentment so prevalent that he was punitive in all things regarding his niece?

"I also wished to pick up willow bark, rose hip, and nettle f-from the alchemist." Beatrice almost seemed to try too hard to explain why she was out and about this morning. "Millborn's rheumatism is acting up, and I want to brew her a t-tea to ease her discomfort."

Once again, Beatrice showed concern for a servant, even to the point of fetching the herbs and brewing tea herself. Cassius admired her intrinsic kindness—something that assuredly wasn't inherent in all the Fairfaxes.

"May I walk with you?" he asked against his better judgment.

Cassius should return to the studio and work. That would be the prudent thing to do. After all, he wasn't a man of independent wealth or leisure. Miss Fairfax's circumstances weren't his business and there was nothing he could do to change them. He certainly couldn't offer her sanctuary nor impose upon his parents to do so as Lucius had with Clodovea.

Still, what harm was there in enjoying a few more minutes of her company and the lovely day?

Beatrice inclined her head, not coyly or flirtatiously, but simply in the affirmative. "As you wish."

Not exactly an enthusiastic response, but neither had she refused.

They walked in silence for a few minutes.

"I owe you an apology, Lord Cassius."

Eyebrows raised, he glanced downward, idly noting the top of her head reached his shoulder. "Whatever for?"

"I was unaccountably rude and unladylike when I departed the other day." Beatrice's delicate jaw tensed, but she stared straight ahead. "I don't know what came over me."

"I took no offense, Miss Fairfax." He grinned and scratched Nala behind her ears. "In fact, it amused me. My sister and grandmother would've applauded your daring. Both enjoy cocking a snook at decorum and strictures."

He almost added, *"I'd like you to meet them someday."* But that was as unlikely and farfetched as portly King George IV climbing atop a horse unassisted or declining a meal.

"They sound delightful." Presenting her profile, Beatrice glanced out over the ocean.

She possessed a perfectly straight nose, delicate and proportional to her features. Another detail his artist mind absently noted.

Something troubled her this morn.

It's none of your business. Do not get involved.

Too late for that.

Cassius had become involved the minute he'd accepted the commission to paint her. A decision he was fast coming to regret. Nothing to do with painting her—for that would be an immense pleasure—but everything to do with what the miniature meant for her future.

He didn't want to contribute to her unhappiness.

It wasn't too late to back out.

He could return the deposit to Highbury.

But what good would that do?

The earl would simply find another artist.

Besides, Cassius *wanted* to paint Beatrice. Wanted to capture her essence and spirit on canvas. *That dimple. Those Freckles. Her heart-shaped face.* He needed to, and that begged the question, *"Why?"*

A sigh slipped past her rose-bud lips.

"I'm not brave or clever or resourceful. If I were, I'd leave my uncle's home and make my way until I turn five and twenty. He doesn't want me there any more than I want to be there." She cut Cassius a swift glance before focusing on the waves once more. "I wonder. Does my staying at Highbury House make me a coward?"

Hands clasped behind his back, Cassius considered her. "No. Not a coward, but wise."

"*Wise?*" Her eyes, turbulent and troubled, she sent him a doubtful sideways glance. "I've never thought so."

"Prudent too." How little Beatrice knew of the world. How unkind and unforgiving it was to women without means. "You told me you don't know anyone who could take you in. How would you manage?"

She was silent for several minutes before murmuring in a defeated tone, "I honestly do not know."

"Exactly so," he said kindly.

A pair of laughing lads in navy and white striped skeleton suits, each holding a kite, raced by.

In the hour Cassius had been on the beach, the shore had filled with tourists and locals wishing to enjoy the sunny day.

"I could be a companion." For a moment, excitement lit Beatrice's freckled features before they fell. "But I don't suppose I could bring my dogs and other pets."

"Probably not." Cassius didn't soften the truth. It wouldn't help her.

The urge to suggest she might find refuge at Hefferwickshire House thrummed against his tongue, but he subdued the improbable conjecture. It was quite possible her husband would deny Beatrice her pets as well.

He'd bite his tongue in half before he spoke those unkind words, however.

Women had so little power in most circumstances.

His parents' union was truly unusual. Father treated Mother as his equal.

"Lord Cassius?" Disillusionment shadowed Beatrice's pretty hazel eyes. "I wonder, how would a person find out what the conditions of an inheritance are?" She jutted her chin out. "I wish to know if I retain control of my trust fund if I marry."

Cassius didn't blame her for wanting to know that very important detail. Her future happiness might well depend upon it.

Eyes narrowed, he rubbed his chin.

"A solicitor would have a copy of the original bequest and likely the trust documents too." She gazed up at him with such trust that his heart turned over. "Do you know the solicitor's name? I could ask my father to make inquiries on your behalf."

She crinkled her nose in concentration. "I don't know for certain, but I've seen correspondences from Hargreaves & Drummond Solicitors on Fleet Street in

London. They might not have anything to do with my trust or inheritance, however."

"That's enough information to start." Cassius gave a satisfied nod. "Who bequeathed the funds to you?"

"My maternal grandmother, Euphemia Fairfax, Countess of Highbury. She died a month after my mother. I don't remember her at all." A precocious smile tilted her pretty mouth upward, replacing the lingering sadness in her eyes. "It always infuriated my uncle that Grandmother didn't disown Mama. He would have inherited my funds had she done so."

Cassius set his jaw against the uncomplimentary reference to an equine's rump her uncle reminded him of.

"Your grandmother loved you despite the circumstances of your birth and wanted to provide for you." How brave and noble of the countess. "Typically, families engage the same solicitor, so there is every chance that the countess retained the same one as your uncle."

Something fluttered behind Cassius's heart again. He could do this for her. Help Beatrice in this small way. It did little to alleviate his guilt, but it was a start.

"I hadn't considered that." She gave a slow nod. "I have asked to see the trust more than once, but my uncle always refuses. He says women shouldn't worry about such matters."

Of course Highbury did, the spawn of Satan.

And why would he do so?

Unless the donkey's hind end was hiding something.

Now, there was an interesting notion.

Cassius would write to Father this very afternoon.

Beatrice switched the dogs' leads to her other hand.

"May I ask something else of you, Lord Cassius?"

"Of course, I shall help if I can."

Warning bells tinkled, but he ignored them. He wasn't getting involved, just helping an unfortunate woman.

"I would like to learn how to best invest my funds." A wry smile tilted her mouth upward. "In general, men aren't keen on advising women regarding such matters, and I have no one else I can ask."

Cassius liked that she spoke with optimism, as if she would come into her inheritance and control it and her future.

She gave him a wry smile. "Women *are* capable of understanding such things, you know."

He chuckled and stepped over a small piece of driftwood. "I do not doubt it in the least. However, that is not my area of expertise. Fletcher and Adolphus are both quite adept at investing, as is my father. I shall write and ask them for suggestions today."

"Thank you. I appreciate your assistance." Her grateful smile momentarily blinded him. "Now, I must go. I've been gone overly long already."

"We can discuss both topics in detail on your next visit

to the studio." Cassius was quite looking forward to spending several hours with her.

A pained, almost desperate expression whisked over her features.

"What is it, Beatrice?"

Her name slipped from Cassius's tongue as if it were the most natural thing in the world, and he could not regret it. Any more than he could regret helping her.

"This morning, my uncle informed me that he met a gentleman at *The Old Ship Hotel* who may be interested in my hand in marriage."

TEN

Highbury House drawing room

THREE DAYS LATER ~ AFTER A VERY AWKWARD SUPPER

Averting her face from the middling-aged, beefy man sitting far too near on the settee, Beatrice took shallow breaths in an ineffective effort to not inhale his stomach-churning stench. What cruel irony that Pemberton Dungworth's breath smelled similar to fresh horse manure.

Sweat beaded his broad brow, balding pate, and thick upper lip, and dampened the armpits of his hideous chartreuse jacket. His fetid breath coming in wheezing pants, he repeatedly dabbed at the moisture with a soggy handkerchief.

"One would expect the temperature to be less stifling with the shore breezes," he complained to no one in particular.

"This is an unusually hot August, and the humidity makes it seem even warmer." Uncle Cedric slid his smug, assessing gaze from Mr. Dungworth to Beatrice and back again. "I trust the weather in Rotherham is more temperate?"

Mr. Dungworth was a partial owner of a successful tannery in Rotherham and now that he'd achieved wealth, he sought a blue-blooded wife to elevate his social status. Only no noblewoman born on the right side of the blanket would consider his suit.

They probably took one whiff and ran hell-bent for nothing in the other direction.

Hence, when he and Uncle Cedric had struck up a conversation at *The Old Ship Hotel* the other night—highly odd that Uncle would deem to lower himself to speak to such a person as Mr. Dungworth—the conversation had drifted toward matrimony.

Or had Uncle steered the discussion in that direction deliberately?

How could he believe Beatrice would ever agree to a match with this odious person?

Every instinct told her that her uncle only considered

Mr. Dungworth's suit for her hand in marriage precisely because the man was so abhorrent.

Was there no end to Uncle Cedric's acrimony?

"However do you manage to appear cool in this oppressive heat, Miss Fairfax?" Daisy, Mr. Dungworth's mother, asked. But before Beatrice could summon a polite response, Mrs. Dungworth wiggled a pudgy finger toward her. "It's the lack of flesh on your bones. Skinny women never understand what we curvaceous women suffer."

Curvaceous?

Beatrice bit the inside of her cheek to prevent her jaw from dropping open.

Neither Mrs. Dungworth's stays nor her son's corset —obvious beneath his jacket—could contain the mother's and son's excess flesh.

As equally corpulent as her offspring, Mrs. Dungworth briskly waved her fan with the vengeance of one attempting to sail a schooner across a windless ocean. Her cheeks heat-reddened, she pulled a face, causing her many chins to fold into one another. "I came to Brighton for the health benefits of sea bathing. However, I can tell you, neither my gout nor arthritis are improved in the least. I also continue to suffer from digestive disorders."

An indiscreet, *loud* passage of wind followed her complaint, but Mrs. Dungworth continued waving her fan without interruption or apology, as if flatulence in drawing rooms was commonplace.

Perhaps for her, it was.

"The cold water makes my joints ache," she said, her tone taking on a whining pitch. "And I vow the breeze is detrimental to my delicate constitution and shall no doubt bring on the ague."

Beatrice would bet a draft horse's constitution was less robust than the matron's.

The hypochondriac hadn't stopped her monologue of pains and illnesses since plopping her broad posterior at the dining table and consuming more rich food than Beatrice had ever witnessed a woman eat.

No wonder she had digestive issues.

"You are sorely tested, to be sure, Mother." Mr. Dungworth gave his mother an indulgent smile. "When I wed, my wife shall tend to your every need. I know how much you look forward to your feet and legs being rubbed each evening to ease the pain from your bunions and gout. You'll no longer have to rely upon a servant to do so. My wife shall do the honors."

Leaning forward, the bull of a man gave Beatrice a speaking glance.

Egads. He cannot be serious.

He expected his wife to rub his mother's feet?

Every night?

Beatrice tried—she really did—not to cast a covert glance at his mother's swollen feet bulging over the tops of her slippers.

Schooling her features into a benign expression, Beatrice lifted her lilac-scented handkerchief to her nose on the pretense of covering a dainty sneeze. A more loathsome pair, she'd never had the misfortune of meeting. For the life of her, she could not conjure a single redeeming quality for either mother or son.

I cannot stand much more of his putrid odor.

As if his malodorous putrid breath wasn't stomach-turning enough, the man reeked of sweat—an onion-like acridity that lingered heavily in the air. A cloying sweet aroma, reminding Beatrice of rotting over-ripe fruit, a cheesy pungency—potent and nauseating—that wafted outward every time he moved, and a sour, yeasty odor that clung to his clothing, made it necessary for her to repeatedly swallow the bile climbing the back of her throat.

The little dinner she had gagged down threatened to reappear.

And still, Uncle Cedric looked on with a cruel air of satisfaction.

Why did he hate her so?

"Shall we take a turn about the terrace, Miss Fairfax?" Mr. Dungworth smiled, revealing a row of yellow, seldom cleaned teeth. "I'm sure the outdoor temperature is more inviting."

"What an excellent notion!" Uncle Cedric exclaimed too enthusiastically while nodding.

Still, outside, Beatrice might avoid a degree of the malodorous assault on her senses.

"Yes, indeed. My dogs would enjoy stretching their legs." If Beatrice must stroll with the repulsive man, at least she'd have her faithful pets nearby should he try anything untoward. "I shall fetch them from my bedchamber."

Uncle had relegated Nala and Teddy to Beatrice's chamber for the evening.

Given how often Mr. Dungworth's bulgy, peat-brown eyes sank to her bosom, she expected he'd not act as the gentleman when they were alone.

Mr. Dungworth scowled. "*I* do not like dogs."

"Horrid, awful creatures," his mother put in. "They scratch and snuffle and smell."

Had she sniffed her son of late?

Or considered the lingering offensiveness of *her* digestive indiscretions?

Beatrice lifted her chin. "My dogs are my closest companions. They go *everywhere* with me."

Nala and Teddy might be the very thing to put this offensive toad off the scent.

"I'm sure the dogs can forfeit a walk this evening, Niece." Steel edged Uncle Cedric's seemingly innocent suggestion. "Mrs. Dungworth and I shall have a nice chat while you enjoy the terrace with Mr. Dungworth."

Rising, Beatrice fashioned a polite smile, though she

wanted to tell her uncle and the Dungworths what she thought of them and damn them to the scorching environment the three of them deserved to spend eternity sweating in. "As you don't intend to act as chaperone, I must insist my dogs accompany me as they do when I walk about Brighton. Otherwise, I shall have to refrain from taking the air. I'm certain no one here would have me smudge my reputation."

Except, Beatrice believed, her uncle didn't give a beggar's curse about her reputation. In fact, he might very well hope Dungworth would compromise her, and then try to force her into marriage with the beastly man afterward.

"Very well." With considerable effort, Mr. Dungworth hoisted his enormous frame from the settee, which creaked in relief upon being spared his immense weight. "I suppose I can manage with the dogs outdoors. Cannot abide them in the house, however."

"Goodness, how ill-suited we are." Beatrice couldn't conceal her triumphant smile, and surely victory glinted in her eyes. "I *sleep* with my pets. Every. Single. Night."

His mouth dropped to his barrel chest as his mother simultaneously exhaled an outraged gasp.

Feeling quite chipper and confident, Beatrice headed toward the doorway, calling over her shoulder, "I shall fetch my dogs and meet you on the terrace, Mr. Dungworth."

Dungworth gave a disgruntled nod and sent Uncle Cedric a blistering glare before trundling toward the open French windows.

Highbury House Terrace

TEN MINUTES LATER

NALA AND TEDDY at her side, Beatrice inhaled a cleansing breath.

This was so much better than inside where odors lingered.

As always, the gentle evening breeze contained a hint of salty tanginess. Nevertheless, compared to the odoriferous man plodding beside her, each breath straining the confines of his corset and making him sound like a winded Ascot racehorse, the breeze was as welcome as a draft from heaven.

"You are attached to the creatures?" Mr. Dungworth gave her dogs an ill-disposed sideways glance.

Beatrice raised an eyebrow. "Yes. Nala and Teddy are like family to me."

Tightening his mouth into a critical line, he made a rough rumbling noise in his throat, which sounded as if he gargled hot coals or glass.

Seizing the opportunity to press her advantage and prove how incompatible they were, she clasped her hands together.

"I am happiest when I am with them. I cannot imagine a life without my pets." She blinked at him innocently. "I also have a blind cat, a fox, a dove, and a hare. Normally, I tend to several more animals as well. I welcome and care for every animal in need."

Dungworth couldn't prevent the revulsion contorting his face but with difficulty, recovered his composure. "*Ahem.* Yes. Well. I view animals purely from a commercial perspective."

The revolting man would.

"We are sorely discordant in that regard." Beatrice didn't mince her words. "I try to save animals, and you make a living from tanning their skins."

His eyes grew marble hard, and his calculating expression made a shudder ripple across her shoulders.

"Miss Fairfax, your uncle gave me permission to address you."

"He overstepped." Beatrice ran a hand over Nala's head to calm and reassure herself. Dungworth was an utter fool if he thought her dogs wouldn't protect her. She lifted her chin. "I am of age and make my own decisions."

Grunting, he shook his beefy head. "His lordship assured me you seek a husband and has, in fact, already selected a church and cleric in London where we are to exchange vows."

London?

That cannot be true.

Before Beatrice could deny the falsehood, Mr. Dungworth suddenly clasped her arm in a bruising grip and forced her to face him. For his immense girth, the man was astonishingly swift.

"You shall require a firm hand, but I believe I can force you into submission eventually." His foul breath gagged Beatrice. "You shall be my wife."

My God in heaven. He's serious.

It was as if he hadn't heard a word she'd said.

Beatrice would not consent to the match.

She would not.

Her life would be utter hell.

Uncle could not force her to wed Mr. Dungworth.

But he *could* toss her onto the street.

He wouldn't do it in Brighton, however. Beatrice was confident of that.

To do so would cast him in a terrible light amongst Brighton's elites, and his reputation was everything to him. Which meant, Uncle Cedric would cart Beatrice elsewhere, where she knew no one and stood no chance of getting help, before he cast her out.

Her stomach gave a sickening jolt as hopelessness rocked her again.

Still, she would rather take her chances on the streets than marry this pig.

"No. I shall not." She thrust her chin upward, proud that she hadn't stuttered once. "I do not know you, nor do I wish to further our acquaintance."

Beatrice tugged ineffectually, trying to free herself. Icy fear slithered up her spine when, instead of heeding her efforts, Dungworth wrapped his other ham-fisted palm around her free arm and jerked her toward him.

Beatrice gasped in pain.

She would bear bruises by tomorrow.

Nala issued a warning growl low in her throat.

Fur raised, Teddy crouched low, prepared to spring to Beatrice's defense.

Stupid, stupid Dungworth, oblivious to the dogs' aggression, dragged Beatrice nearer and attempted a slobbery kiss. She quickly averted her face, his fat, wet lips skidding across her cheek to her ear, leaving a putrid saliva trail on her skin.

"How d-dare you?" She wrested a hand free and slapped him with all her strength, the sound echoing in the still evening. "I shall n-never marry you. Never!"

Nala lunged and Teddy dove.

The boarhound clamped her jaws on Dungworth's

ample behind as Teddy sank his sharp teeth into the fiend's calf.

Howling in pain, Dungworth promptly released Beatrice's other arm and cupped his portly rump with one hand and his calf with the other.

"Now I understand why no man will have you, and why your uncle cannot wait to be rid of you," he growled between his stained teeth. "You'll end up a dried-up spinster."

"Far better than tied to a slovenly, obese wretch for life."

She turned and ran to her bedchamber, dogs at her heels, and locked the door behind her.

Leaning against the wood panel, her heart pounding in her throat and hands clammy with fear-induced sweat, Beatrice closed her eyes.

What have I done?

ELEVEN

Sussex Square ~ Kempton

*FIVE DAYS LATER ~ ALMOST TEN IN THE
MORNING*

Sighing, Cassius finished his coffee, then set the empty cup on a nearby side table.

Beatrice had missed her last sitting.

As he scraped a hand through his already tousled hair, concern for her chafed him. Particularly after she'd disclosed that Highbury might have found a potential husband for her right here in Brighton.

Her note explaining her absence informed him Millborn ailed and it wouldn't be proper for Beatrice to come for a sitting without a chaperone. She would come today instead.

A reasonable excuse. And yet, Cassius couldn't help but wonder if her uncle meant to force her into a union with this unnamed man, thereby forgoing the need to finish the painting.

He'd taken it upon himself to snoop around *The Old Ship Hotel* to see if he could discover who the potential suitor was. However, he lacked his brother Lucius's and cousin Torrian's sleuthing skills, and his questions only earned him skeptically raised eyebrows and uncooperative frowns from the staff and patrons.

He sent another fretful glance to the studio's front window.

Sun glistened off the ocean, a perfect backdrop to the clear sapphire sky.

No shiny burgundy coach trundled down the cobbled lane. Interesting that Highbury chose such an arresting color for his conveyance rather than the typical noble black preferred by most peers.

Exhaling a deep breath, Cassius scratched his neck as his attention dropped to the letters that had arrived yesterday. He'd wanted to charge straight to Highbury House and share the contents with Beatrice, but wisdom and prudence warned him not to.

Instead, he'd penned letters to his father and Adolphus, asking them to come to Brighton at their earliest convenience. Not only was the Earl of

Highbury in debt up to his perfectly starched and tied neckcloth, but he was also on the verge of bankruptcy.

The earl must not learn what Cassius had discovered until he was positive Beatrice was safe. And at present, he didn't believe she was, though he wouldn't want to alarm her unnecessarily.

From the moment he'd met the Earl of Highbury, Cassius suspected something about the man was off, but had dismissed his initial aversion as being unfair and judgmental.

Next time, Cassius would listen to his gut instinct.

Regardless, if Beatrice didn't come for her sitting today, Cassius would contrive an excuse to either call at Highbury House or send a note around asking her to meet him at The Chapel Royal, where he attended Sunday services—mainly because that was where his parents went when in Brighton.

A guinea greasing a palm would ensure discreet delivery of the missive without the earl's knowledge.

At last, Highbury's gleaming coach drew to a halt before his studio, and he released a sigh of relief.

Beatrice emerged from the carriage's interior, and not waiting for Hampton to hand her down, gracefully hopped onto the pavement.

Millborn did not appear in the doorway.

Nala bounded from the conveyance and with a happy

woof, darted through the studio's open door to give Cassius an excited greeting.

"Hello, girl." He rubbed her ears.

Beatrice lifted Teddy, and holding him to her chest with one arm, shaded her eyes with her other hand as she glanced upward at Hampton.

"Return at the usual time, please."

"Your uncle bid me fetch you home at 1:00 today, Miss." Hampton's weathered features crumpled into an apologetic smile.

"He did?" Confusion whisked across her pretty face. "Did he say why?"

The driver shook his head. "No, Miss."

"Very well." She produced a sunny smile. "I shall see you then."

Did Beatrice realize she rarely stuttered when her uncle wasn't present?

She entered the studio, and her chest rose with the deep breath she took.

"Good morning, Beatrice."

Cassius drank her in, his jaded soul parched and dry.

A long time ago, before he'd hardened his heart, he might have had room in it for her.

"Good morning." She blinked as her eyes adjusted to the darker interior. She gave a little sniff. "I like the smell of your studio, Lord Cassius."

Unusual, but it made him glad.

"I hoped that by now you would call me Cassius, Beatrice."

He stroked Nala's broad head.

Eyes half-closed, and leaning into his thigh, the large dog gave a contented sigh.

"I vow, she has fallen in love with you...Cassius."

Stupid though it was, his soul soared when Beatrice complied with his simple request.

Teddy wiggled in her arms, and she put him down. "This chap as well."

The one-eyed dog made straight for Cassius and demanded a pet too.

After Cassius picked him up and gave him a hearty greeting, he strode toward Beatrice.

"No Millborn today?" He tried not to stare as she untied her silk cloak and her glorious hair billowed around her slender shoulders.

Upon seeing the angry yellowish-green bruises on her upper arms, he clenched his jaw.

Fiend seize it!

How had she come by the marks?

Had Highbury resorted to physical brutality?

By God, the cur had better not have.

"No." Despair tightened the corners of Beatrice's face and drew her pretty mouth downward. "Her health has not improved. In truth, I fear her condition worsens. The cough has settled in her chest, and she has become so weak, she cannot leave her bed."

She managed a sad, nascent smile, and Cassius's heart flopped over.

"She's been my companion since childhood," Beatrice said. "And I confess that I'm afraid for her."

No doubt for herself as well.

Surely she suffered from loneliness, and the potential loss of her companion must weigh heavily upon her.

He'd have to be blind not to notice.

"Has a physician been to see her?" If not, Cassius would arrange for one to do so promptly.

"Yes." Beatrice nodded before drifting farther into the room, then pulling a face. "The old quack merely prescribed a tonic, which smelled mostly of alcohol and laudanum. I've been putting poultices on Millborn's chest and having her drink eucalyptus tea to help break up the congestion, but neither appears to be helping."

"I have a doctor friend, Lawrence Lancaster, in Brighton," Cassius said. "He works at Sussex County Hospital and is trained in all the newest methodologies. I shall ask him to look in on her."

"Would you?" Such appreciation shone in Beatrice's eyes that it momentarily took his breath away. "I would appreciate it ever so much."

"I'm surprised your uncle permitted you to come today without a chaperone." In point of fact, that wasn't entirely true. Nothing Highbury did would surprise

Cassius after what he'd recently learned about the unscrupulous earl.

Expression shuttered, Beatrice firmed her lips into a tight ribbon.

"He's quite angry with me. I don't think he gives two farthings about my reputation anymore." She lifted a shoulder, a tiny triumphant smile touching the corners of her mouth. "I rejected the man he chose for me to marry."

Cassius shouldn't care a jot, so why did he want to whoop for joy?

"Oh?" Resting his hips on his desk, he folded his arms, resisting the temptation to draw her into his embrace and tell her how proud he was of her for standing up to her bully of an uncle. "Why do I think there is more to the story?"

Her lips twitched. "Nala might have bitten Mr. Dungworth on the bottom."

"Dung—?" Cassius choked on a guffaw. "*Dungworth*?"

"Indeed, of Dungworth and Babinet Leatherworks." She wrinkled her nose. "And his breath smelled of horse manure." A giggle escaped her; an unfettered expression of joy. "I also slapped him for trying to force a kiss on me, and Teddy bit his calf."

Ire, unlike anything Cassius had ever experienced, burned through his veins. Was that blackguard the reason for the bruises on her arms? Mustering calm he was far from feeling, he gave an approving nod.

"Bravo Teddy and Nala, and well done you!"

At once dismay transformed Beatrice's features.

She met Cassius's eyes, despair in hers. "He was a horrid man with an equally horrid mother. They smelled as if they'd never touched a bar of soap in their lives. What is more, they expected me to rub her bunions and gouty feet and legs every night."

Shock rendered him speechless for an instant as he tried to digest that bit of offensiveness. "Surely not."

"Moreover, they detest dogs. I'm positive Mr. Dungworth would not have permitted me my pets had I accepted his oafish offer. Not that I considered it at all." She shook her head, that curtain of burnished gold and copper, swaying about her shoulders. "Uncle has barely spoken to me since. Except to say we are back to the original plan."

She slid a glance at the covered canvas.

"Which is that once I finish the miniature, he'll journey to London to find a husband for you." His stomach having gone sour, Cassius set Teddy down.

"Yes." Beatrice no longer sounded defeated, but simply resigned to the facts.

She cocked her head.

"Cassius, may I ask you something personal?"

"Why is it I think you will whether I agree or not?"

Enjoying their banter, he permitted a teasing smile. "You may, but I don't have to answer."

"Ah, you are being sly." She shook a finger at him, laughter dancing in her eyes. "Let me rephrase, then. Will you answer a personal question?"

He should say no, but even as the thought shot through his mind, Cassius nodded.

"If you could change anything about your life and experiences, what would it be?"

Zounds, Beatrice went straight to the core of things, didn't she?

Neck bent, he cupped his nape and considered her question.

"My first instinct is to wish I had never met Constanza."

How many times had he said those very words?

"It would've saved me untold heartache, but when I reflect on my journey as an artist, I don't believe I would be where I am today had I not had that experience." He shrugged. "Time might not heal all wounds, but it does smooth out the edges and creates a buffer so one can go on and be happy."

"*Are* you happy?" Beatrice searched his face with those enormous hazel eyes.

What did she seek?

"That's *two* questions, snoopy miss." He held up two fingers. "My turn."

Shaking her head, unease replacing her earlier comradery, Beatrice retreated a couple of paces. "I didn't agree—"

"Do not tell me you don't play fair, Beatrice Fairfax." Grinning, Cassius leaned forward. "Tit for tat. What's good for the goose is good for the gander. Turnabout is fair play."

"*Hmph.*" Arms folded, she pressed her pretty lips together. "Very well, but I shall not promise to answer if you are too prying."

"I'll ask you the same question you asked me." Cassius was genuinely curious about her response. "If you could change anything about *your* life, what would it be?"

A faraway look entered her eyes as she stared out the window. "That my mother had lived."

Cassius had expected her to answer that she'd been born legitimate.

His heart twinged with compassion.

He'd grown up with supportive, doting, loving parents.

Beatrice knew nothing of that kind of unconditional love.

She also wouldn't be in the precarious position she found herself in today had she not been orphaned at a young age and left in the Earl of Highbury's questionable care.

Sadness shadowed the smile she summoned. "I

suppose we ought to start. Hampton is returning an hour early today, although I don't know why."

Hopefully not another attempt by her blackguard uncle to introduce Beatrice to a potential suitor.

"Yes, well. Before we get to that, Beatrice, I have news for you."

Her hazel eyes widened. "Oh?"

"I received letters from my father and brothers yesterday." Cassius picked up a short stack of missives from his desk.

He lifted the first.

"Adolphus recommends investing in shipping, trade, and textiles. No surprise there. He owns a ship, and he's open to discussing a venture with you."

"He is?" Excitement lit Beatrice's face. "That would be wonderful."

"Indeed." Cassius tossed the first letter on the desk and waved another folded rectangle. "Fletcher suggests investing in real estate and, though in their infancy, railways."

"Railways?" Beatrice touched a slender finger to her dimpled chin. "I've never seen a train. Do you suppose they will grow in popularity? I imagine they would be quite useful for transporting goods."

Cassius shrugged. "I'm not certain I'm altogether keen on tracks cutting through landscapes, affecting agriculture and wildlife, or the noise and polluted air they would cause. But I am pragmatic and suspect railways are the way of the future for products and passengers."

"Yes, I think you may be right." Setting aside her cloak, she nodded. "That is, if I *can* invest my inheritance. I'm positive that my uncle shall not wait until I'm five and twenty. He is desperate to be rid of me. I fear he may try to force me to wed, by fair means or foul."

Face flushed, she laced her fingers together, but Cassius saw her trembling hands.

"Bollocks to that!"

He slapped his thigh with his free hand with such vehemence that she jumped.

Nala's ears perked up, and she gazed at him, her brown eyes worried.

"I don't know precisely why your uncle is rushing you down the aisle." Tension thrummed through his veins as Cassius lifted the last letter. "However, Father uncovered some *very* interesting information regarding your trust and inheritance."

Beatrice raised her red-blonde eyebrows, a glimmer of hope lighting her eyes. "Such as?"

"Perhaps you should sit down." Cassius motioned toward the settee.

Her eyebrows rose higher on her forehead, and she jutted out that adorable, stubborn chin.

"Have you learned nothing about me, Lord Cassius

Westbrook? I am not a wilting flower who will swoon or give into hysterics."

A reluctant grin twitched the corners of his mouth. "No, you most certainly are not."

She glanced out the large front window and smiled when she spotted two young women walking past.

Their eyes rounded, and they waved at her.

Beatrice returned their friendly greeting before they dipped their heads together, no doubt speaking about her.

"Friends of yours?" Cassius came to stand beside her.

"Yes. Esme Dawkins and Charlotte Hawthorne." She twirled a lock of hair. "In truth, my only friends in Brighton. I told them you are painting my portrait and the reason. They sympathize with my plight, but as the daughter of a local vicar and granddaughter to a widow, they have no means to assist me."

Nor would they dare cross the earl.

There was more to the devious man than his immaculate grooming and noble façade. It seems Highbury had a reputation for assuring he had his way.

Turning away from the window, Beatrice cocked her head. "So what did the duke discover? I assume Hargreaves & Drummond Solicitors was a successful lead?"

Cassius tried to subdue the consternation he was certain Beatrice could see on his face. What he had to say would alarm her—probably frighten her as well. He cupped her shoulders. It was bold and mad of him, but he needed to assure her with more than mere words.

He was here for her—would champion and protect her.

"More so than you could imagine, Beatrice."

Her eyes clear and guileless, she searched his face. "Now I am most curious."

How to tell her?

He clenched his jaw for half a second.

Straightforward and direct.

That was what she would want.

"Beatrice, you were to come into your inheritance either when you married or when you turned one and twenty. Whichever came first. You've been eligible to claim your funds for some time now."

TWELVE

"I beg your pardon?" Beatrice's eyes widened, and she paled, her freckles standing out in stark contrast against her ivory skin. "One and twenty? *Not* five and twenty?"

Though his news had visibly rocked her, she stood strong and confident.

So much strength and determination.

Cassius admired her all the more because of her stalwartness.

He couldn't refrain from giving her shoulders a comforting squeeze, then stepped away before he threw caution to the wind and drew her into his arms as he longed to do. "You've been able to claim your inheritance all this time. The solicitors have sent multiple correspondences to you asking why you have not done so."

"Correspondences, my uncle intercepted, no doubt." Bitterness at her uncle's duplicity leached into her whispered response.

"There's more." Despite Cassius's common sense telling him to tread carefully, to not touch her again, he tilted her chin upward with his forefinger.

"I'm not sure my constitution can handle any more shocks today, Cassius," she quipped, although her low tone held a note of sincerity and guardedness.

"This news will please you. You're not inheriting twenty thousand pounds. Your trust funds were invested wisely, and you have more than fifty-five thousand pounds, Beatrice."

Gasping, she slapped a palm over her mouth, her eyes enormous with disbelief.

"You are a wealthy woman. Furthermore, your husband does not gain control when you marry. The monies remain yours." Father had double-checked those unusual stipulations. "Your grandmother was a clever woman, for if you died before claiming your inheritance, the funds would've passed to a charity to care for unfortunate women like your mother."

The dowager had ensured her son would not get the funds, but why?

Because she'd loved her daughter, despite the scandal surrounding her?

Because she knew what a scapegrace her son was?

"I d-don't understand." Looking utterly dazed, Beatrice shook her head. "Why would Uncle Cedric lie to me? He could have been rid of me last year. Why hide the truth from me?"

"That is what I mean to find out."

Cassius traced his thumb over her jaw.

Petal soft.

She stood, transfixed.

Would the rest of her be as velvety smooth?

He couldn't tear his focus from her plump lips. Just inches away, they beckoned to him like cool water to a parched man in the desert.

One kiss.

What could one kiss hurt?

Bollocks, man.

Cease your infernal romantic speculation.

He cleared his throat, deliberately breaking the spell. "Tell me about your uncle's finances."

Beatrice blinked as if awakened from a daze, then wrinkled her nose like an adorable bunny.

"I honestly don't know anything about them. He's stingy about some things, but not anything that has to do with keeping up appearances. Nevertheless, he makes me pay for my wardrobe and the care of my animals with a small allowance from my trust fund."

That didn't come as a surprise.

Cassius suspected the earl wasn't as flush in the pockets as he pretended, and that was worth investigating. In truth, Cassius had already written to his brother Lucius, requesting he do just that. He believed the earl had been plotting to get his greedy hands on her funds, or at least a portion of them, one way or another, for some time.

Though how, given the former countess' provisions, Cassius couldn't imagine. Moreover, why had Highbury waited until now?

Likely, the earl had come up with the scheme to see Beatrice wed because he'd lied to her about the age she could inherit, and he'd hoped the guise of a forced marriage would keep that little detail hidden.

His lordship hadn't counted on Beatrice's resourcefulness or tenacity.

Her eyelids fluttered closed, her gold-tipped lashes brushing the tops of her cheeks.

When she opened them, resolution had replaced her earlier shock, though she still appeared a trifle piqued. No doubt due to the strain of worrying about her sick companion, fretting about the earl's motives, and the discomfit of having to deal with the likes of Mr. Dungworth.

Lord, how Cassius admired her pluck.

"I know it's a lot to ask, b-but will you take me to

London to m-meet with the solicitor?" Her expression held such hope. "I can p-pay you for your trouble after I receive my inheritance."

"I don't want your money, Beatrice."

In fact, her offer insulted him, though he knew she hadn't intended for it to.

"I meant n-no offense, Cassius." A flush stole up her face, but she persisted. "*Will* you take me to London? Please?"

Cassius should refuse—not even consider helping her for half a second.

I shall regret getting involved.

Too bloody bad.

I'm already involved.

He'd become involved the minute he accepted the commission to paint her likeness.

No, he became captivated the instant he saw her running across the lawn at Highbury House.

Two entirely different things.

"I shan't take you to London, but I shall take you to Hefferwickshire House, the ducal estate, and with my father, we can all journey to the city." Not only would her uncle expect them to head straight for London, but Cassius wanted the protection his father could provide if they encountered Highbury in the city.

Cassius cupped her face, her soft lips mere inches away. "But we must leave now."

"*Now?*" she choked, going pale as chalk again. "I c-cannot. What about M-Millborn? My other animals?"

"I'm positive the solicitors have written your uncle regarding Father's inquiries." In point of fact, that might be the reason Highbury demanded Beatrice return earlier today—to confront her. "If we don't go now, you might not find another opportunity, and I believe you are no longer safe in your uncle's care. I'll have my doctor friend look in on Millborn."

Cassius glanced out the window.

Even now, did someone watch his establishment, spying on Beatrice?

"Do you ride?" he asked.

"No." She shook her head. "Uncle wouldn't permit me to learn."

She sneezed, then sneezed again before retrieving a plain square from her reticule and, half-turning away, blew her nose.

Cassius stifled his curse.

That meant they must travel by coach, which was much slower progress and easier for Highbury to catch up, as they must take the typical routes, rather than shortcuts only a horse could manage.

Beatrice had arrived almost a half hour ago. They'd only have about two hours head start before Hampton arrived to pick her up.

Already, it might be too late. The journey would

take two to three days, and that was if they had a four-horse team, changed horses every fifteen miles, and only stopped to sleep for no more than eight hours.

"Is there no one who can care for your other animals?" he asked.

"Yes." She nodded, her face still pale as milk except for two bright pink spots on her freckled cheeks. "Hans. The cook's grandson."

"Can he read?"

If they stood any chance of outsmarting Highbury, they must leave post haste, but Cassius knew Beatrice well enough to know that she would not abandon her companion or pets.

"Yes." She wadded the handkerchief in her palm, a telltale sign of her agitation.

Cassius hurried to his desk and pulled out a sheet of foolscap. He pushed an inkwell and pen toward her. "Write him a note. Only ask him to care for your animals. Don't tell him *anything* else."

"Of course." Nodding, she took the pen.

Cassius grabbed a second pen and swiftly wrote a short message to Doctor Lawrence Lancaster.

After folding her note to Hans, she met his gaze.

He took her hand in his, and she clasped his tightly, seeming to need his strength.

"It shall not be an easy or comfortable journey,

Beatrice. We might not be able to outrun your uncle if he decides to pursue us." Cassius honestly didn't know if the earl would or not, but if Highbury had lied to Beatrice all this time, what else was the earl capable of?

She merely pressed her lips together and gave a single curt nod.

"Your reputation will be in shreds after traveling alone with me." He must tell her the rest—make certain there would be no misunderstandings or false assumptions. "And I shan't be making an offer of marriage."

She didn't even flinch at his callous announcement, and Cassius couldn't decide if that made him admire her even more or saddened him.

It didn't matter that his actions would be beyond reproach. A young, unmarried woman traveling alone with a man was scandalous. Many a man had been compelled to marry a chit compromised far less than Beatrice would be after their hasty journey.

"My reputation is the least of my worries, and I wouldn't accept a m-marriage offer from you, or any man for that matter. I have no wish to marry. Ever." Her posture grew stiffer with each word. "So you can rest easy on that account."

What a pair they were—both averse to marriage.

She offered him a fragile smile. "Besides, I trust you to act the gentleman."

As long as her trust didn't turn into something more, for Cassius had sworn an oath to himself he would not break. Which was why he'd made certain to inform her he'd not be salvaging her reputation by trotting down the aisle.

He helped her on with her cloak—entirely too identifiable, but he didn't have another to offer her instead. Once they were on their way, he'd purchase more suitable and less noticeable clothing for her.

"We go now." Chin held high, she snapped her fingers. At once, her faithful dogs trotted to her side. "Today, I take control of my life and future."

"Bravo, Beatrice."

Surely the sensation pelting Cassius's ribs was pride and admiration—nothing more, and certainly nothing as stupid and senseless as affection.

After securing the front door, he removed his money from a locked desk drawer, tucked it inside an inner coat pocket, and bundled Beatrice out the rear entrance, the letters for Hans and Dr. Lancaster in his hand.

He sent an ironic glance heavenward.

A fine mess I've embroiled myself in.

Of all his siblings, he was the most sensible.

Everyone said so.

Then why was he jumping headlong into this insane escapade?

Because, dammit, despite his best intentions, and

though he'd fought it from the first time he'd laid eyes upon Beatrice Fairfax, she'd managed to wiggle her way beneath his skin, and he very much feared, was well on her way to burrowing into his heart.

And that he must put a stop to it at once.

THIRTEEN

*On the track between Brighton
and Cumberland, England
Near The Frolicking Fox Inn*

*A DAY LATER ~ A FEW MINUTES PAST NINE IN
THE EVENING*

Stroking Teddy's soft fur, Beatrice gazed at the passing landscape. Dusk had settled on the countryside, a comforting blue-gray mantle deepening the forest shadows. Nala lay curled on the floor, snoring softly. As the miles passed and Brighton grew more distant, Beatrice hadn't dared relax, but the tension knotting her stomach and shoulders had eased somewhat.

Though she hadn't breathed a word to Cassius, he

realized she'd caught Millborn's cold. So far, Beatrice's symptoms proved more of an annoyance than a worry. A sore throat, sneezing, and a stuffy nose plagued her, but not the bone-rattling cough, weakness, and fever her companion suffered.

Last night, Beatrice and Cassius hadn't stopped to sleep—only to eat, change horses several times, and procure her the too-big and unremarkable dark blue gown, black cloak, and black bonnet with a veil that she wore to hide her identity. He had also purchased several squares for her to blow her leaking nose into.

She'd braided her hair and wound it into a knot at the back of her head, but she didn't have any pins to secure it in place, so strands kept slipping loose. The color was unique enough that she needed to keep it hidden beneath the hideous bonnet.

Cassius hadn't thought to acquire hairpins for her, but after she removed her bonnet for at least the sixth time and re-braided her hair, he'd used a knife to cut away a long strip of lace trailing down the back of the bonnet.

Beatrice had wound the lace around her head in a makeshift turban and tied it at the top before replacing the ugly hat once more.

They traveled as a bereaved brother and sister.

If anyone caught a glimpse of her, they might attribute her sniffles to tears, instead of a cold, reinforcing their ruse.

That charade had been Cassius's idea. One he said he borrowed from a brother, though he didn't expound on which sibling or what story lay behind the ruse. Perhaps she would find out when they reached Hefferwickshire House.

She eyed him covertly.

Perhaps not.

Though courteous and kind, Cassius seemed to have withdrawn into himself on the journey. He barely spoke and seemed distracted. She supposed the stress and tension of fleeing Brighton and the worry that Uncle Cedric might overtake them could have caused the change in Cassius. Probably concerns about his career plagued him too.

Though there'd always been an aura of seriousness about him, Beatrice missed the easy-to-talk-to man.

She'd had no right to overstep and impose upon him the way she had, and guilt nagged her conscience for embroiling him in her mess.

While other men might have denied her appeal without a second thought, Cassius Westbrook was a true gentleman. He held himself to a higher standard and would not dismiss her outlandish request.

Mayhap he had regrets.

She couldn't blame him.

He'd ordered the horses changed every ten miles instead of fifteen to keep them fresh and able to travel at a faster pace. At great expense too. The coach made for an uncomfortable bed, though exhaustion had eventually claimed her in the wee morning hours.

A cramp in her neck had awoken her. All day, her muscles had protested the confined quarters and lack of movement.

How much worse must it be for a tall man such as Cassius?

Fatigue etched his handsome face and pinched the corners of his brilliant eyes, midnight blue, in the coach's dim interior.

Unlike her fitful dozing, he'd remained awake to direct the coachmen along lesser-known roads. He also explained they were less likely to be set upon by highwaymen since knights of the road preyed upon vehicles traveling the more popular routes.

More than once, Beatrice had asked herself why he would go to such an extent to help someone he barely knew or, for that matter, why she'd felt she could ask him to aide her.

No answer presented itself for the former, but the latter was obvious.

Because she *did* trust him.

Had done so from the moment he'd turned from the folly at Highbury House and given her that disarmingly crooked smile.

She hid a yawn behind her hand.

Lord, she'd never been so exhausted, and to think they had at least two more days of this rugged journey ahead of them nearly made her weep.

Nearly.

But she would not.

Not even when the annoying summer cold made her want to curl up in bed and sleep for a week.

You are made of sterner stuff, Beatrice Blossom Carina Fairfax.

If this was what she must endure to free herself from Uncle Cedric's clutches at long last, then she would travel for a fortnight or longer under these grueling conditions.

"I'll rent two rooms tonight." Cassius's murmured comment pulled her attention back to the present. "You can bathe, eat, and sleep for a few hours."

A hot bath to wash the sweat and road grime away sounded divine.

He rubbed a hand across his forehead, weariness etched upon his handsome features. "We'll leave well before dawn. I'll ask for enough food to last the day."

Unless Beatrice had needed to use the necessary behind the inns that they'd stopped at to switch teams, she'd remained out of sight in the stifling vehicle. So had the dogs. The coach paused along the route to allow her pets to relieve themselves. The fewer people who saw her or the dogs, the better.

She fingered the ill-fitting gown.

Cassius had burned her other garments during one of their stops for the dogs.

Beatrice didn't want to contemplate how much he had spent on her behalf.

Of course, she'd reimburse him and pay for the inconvenience she'd caused him as well, even if the stubborn man insisted she need not. *When* she finally controlled the fortune coming to her, that was.

A little thrill of excitement and hope sluiced through her at the thought.

She was wealthy.

Very wealthy and on her way to claiming her inheritance. And there wasn't a blasted thing Uncle Cedric could do to stop her from acquiring what was legally hers.

Except prevent her from meeting with her solicitor.

This begged the question, why would he do so?

But then again, why had he lied and sabotaged her for the last couple of years?

Over and over, she'd ruminated about the reasons Uncle Cedric could have had for lying to her about her inheritance. His behavior made no sense. Initially, she'd believed he'd kept her from her bequest out of spite, but then why the sudden urgency to see her married?

Beatrice's husband wouldn't inherit either, which made Uncles desperation to see her married all the more confounding. Surely, Uncle Cedric was acquainted with the provisions of his mother's will and the legacy she'd left to Beatrice.

Nala lifted her head and giving Beatrice a soulful glance, yawned.

The dogs had suffered from the cramped quarters too, though not nearly as much as Cassius with his long legs. He'd not grumbled once, but then she'd learned that much about him. He wasn't the complaining sort.

"We're nearly to The Frolicking Fox, Beatrice."

She almost asked him to call her BeBe, but that seemed far too personal and intimate.

Cassius flicked a paint-stained finger toward her hat. "Lower the veil and keep your head down when we enter."

He returned his perusal to the road ahead.

As if sensing they were about to stop, Teddy hopped off her lap and stretched, first his back legs, then his front.

A frown tugged Beatrice's mouth downward.

"Cassius?"

"*Hmm?*" he gave her a distracted glance.

"My d-dogs are sure to give us away. How will we g-get them inside without anyone noticing?"

He swung his gaze between the animals.

Their flight would've been easier without her beloved pets. Yet he'd never suggested she leave them behind.

"Leave it to me. They'll stay in the coach for now. After dark, I'll walk them and see if I can bribe someone to let me sneak them up a back stairway." He patted Nala's head. "However, they might have to spend the night in the coach. If that is the case, I'll stay with them."

That hardly seemed fair, but what alternative was there?

A woman sleeping in a coach would arouse too much notice, and she risked being set upon by unscrupulous riffraff.

"My poor dears. Look what I've dragged you into, loves." At least they were with her, and as much as Beatrice hated leaving them for the night, she couldn't argue with Cassius's logic. No one must notice them, and Nala especially, was hard to hide.

Hopefully, Dr. Lancaster had visited Millborn by now.

She frowned.

Would Uncle Cedric permit it?

A few minutes later, the coach slowed to a bumpy stop before a quaint two-story Tudor-style inn. Golden light glowed from the lower windows, framed by brown shutters, and one upper room as well. What must be the stables parallelled one side of the tidy courtyard.

As Beatrice had never traveled before, she did not know if this establishment was typical for lodging. It mattered not in any event. This is where they would sleep tonight.

The coachmen couldn't go on either, though they took turns at the reins.

Cassius put a finger to his lips to indicate she should remain quiet before he jumped from the conveyance and shut the door firmly behind him. He murmured a few indistinguishable words to the drivers before sauntering toward the lodging house, his keen gaze taking in the surroundings as he went.

Several minutes passed—just enough time for her imagination to start to run amuck.

A trio of men passed by, their unassuming clothing revealing them as commoners. They spoke in low tones, and she shrank into the vehicle's shadows.

Nala issued a low growl and Teddy's ears perked up.

"*Shh.*" Beatrice ran a hand over each of their heads. "*Quiet.*"

They knew that command well, for she'd made certain Uncle Cedric could never complain the dogs were too noisy to be in the house. Both dogs promptly settled their head on their forepaws, their faithful gazes trained upon her.

Daring to lean forward to peek out the window, Beatrice only saw one other nondescript coach in the courtyard. However, several horses milled about a corral adjacent to the stables.

Cassius had said this route was less traveled than the Great North Road when weighing whether speed or secrecy was their greatest concern. He'd settled on somewhere in between. Tomorrow, they'd reach the major route and make for Hefferwickshire House hell-bent for nothing.

His words, not hers.

After closing her eyes, Beatrice rested her head against the gray velvet squabs and let her mind wander to what she would do first after she claimed her fortune.

Retrieve my other animals from Highbury House and set up a sanctuary.

Retire Millborn to a cozy cottage.

Find a place to live—not in Brighton.

Not as long as Uncle Cedric lived there. Especially now that she knew the truth of his deception. That meant she wouldn't see Cassius anymore, and her heart panged with sadness and regret.

She *really* liked him. A lot. He'd become a trusted friend—maybe something more.

He cannot be anything more, you gullible goose.

FOURTEEN

Inside the stale and stuffy coach

ABOUT FIFTEEN MINUTES LATER

Beatrice would miss the ocean, the waves rushing ashore, the tang in the air, the call of the gulls... Mayhap she would find a house in another seashore town, if not in England, then perhaps France or Italy.

She'd dozed off when Cassius's urgent whisper dragged her from Morpheus's arms.

"Beatrice?"

"*Hmm?*"

She didn't want to wake up.

The effort to stir and walk inside the inn overwhelmed

her. Her head felt stuffed with wool, her tongue as if goats had tromped around inside her mouth after frolicking in muck, and her throat burned with a fierceness that rivaled gargling with hot coals. Her cold had worsened, not improved.

"Hurry, Beatrice." A hint of impatience, or perchance worry, threaded Cassius's urgent command.

Beatrice touched her dogs on their heads and whispered, "Stay quiet."

They would obey.

Nala also made for an excellent guard.

"There's a back entrance." Cassius reached in and took her hand to help her down. He spoke low, near her ear. "I explained you were overcome with grief and didn't wish anyone to see you in such a distraught state."

Beatrice liked his voice. Not too deep or rough, but a pleasant, melodic baritone.

Focus, you goose.

With concentrated effort, she shook off her whimsical musing.

They hadn't discussed *who* they grieved for. An oversight they should remedy sooner rather than later so that their stories correlated if necessary.

She nodded, for he'd already warned her not to speak.

"We've had a bit of unexpected luck. My eldest half-brother, Layton, is here."

She formed a surprised "O" with her mouth.

Cassius gave her a sideways smile, though there was no humor in the upward sweep of his well-molded mouth. "Layton was on his way to Brighton, to see me. He's a former captain in His Majesty's Army, and I don't mind telling you, I'm relieved to have encountered him. He's armed and has agreed to accompany us the rest of the way to Hefferwickshire."

Beatrice nodded again, grateful they'd have an ally and curious about this other Westbrook brother.

Placing her hand onto Cassius's forearm, she couldn't help but notice the taut muscles rippling and flexing beneath her fingertips. Though she was loath to admit it, she didn't feel at all well and welcomed his support and strength as he led her to a back entrance, up a flight of sturdy steps, and down a dimly lit corridor—the lower half of the walls covered in wainscotting—until they came to a room at the end of the passage.

"This is your room." He indicated a door.

A wood square displayed a tidy number six in red paint above her chamber.

He jutted his firm chin to the door on the right.

Number five.

"That's mine. They have connecting doors. I thought that wisest in case something unforeseen occurs." He pointed to a door across and down the passageway. "Layton's chamber is just down the corridor."

She gave a weary nod.

The truth was, she might not be able to stay awake to eat and bathe. Her head throbbed, every muscle in her body ached, and a tightness had invaded her chest.

"I've asked for our meal to be sent up and then for baths afterward. I'll check on the dogs before and after." He dug in his coat pocket and fished around before withdrawing a skeleton key. "I also paid a stable lad a hefty sum to keep their presence a secret."

Nala and Teddy weren't his responsibility, yet Cassius hadn't exhibited a qualm about looking after them. She'd always thought the manner in which a man—any person for that matter—cared for animals said much about their character.

He inserted the key into the lock. It made a slight scraping noise as he turned it and then toed the door open with his boot. Ribbons of light from the corridor filtered into the dark room.

Leaving her standing just inside the entrance, he crossed to a table where he lit a candle, revealing a clean, if somewhat stark, chamber. A bed covered in a dark green bedspread dominated the small room. In the far corner, a washstand held a porcelain basin and pitcher, a towel, a bar of soap, and a chamber pot on the lower shelf. A single high-back chair sat beneath a window next to the table upon which the candle flickered.

"Stay in here and do not open the door for anyone unless I'm in the room too." Cassius crossed back to Beatrice, searching her face. He pulled back her veil and touched her cheek with the knuckle of his bent forefinger, his expression tender.

As it had yesterday, his attention lingered on her mouth, and Beatrice was fairly certain he battled an urge to kiss her. What was more, she wanted him to lose that inner struggle.

Just once, so she would know a man's kiss before she became a dried-up prune of a spinster.

Not any man's kiss.

Only Cassius's kiss would do.

Foolish girl.

She pulled a face at her silly ruminations.

He must have mistaken the contortion for an objection to the restrictions he imposed, for a muscle flexed in his jaw. Just as well, for Beatrice would die of humiliation should he ever become aware of her silly fantasies.

"I know these measures seem extreme, Beatrice, but we cannot be too careful. I'll bring my brother to meet you later if I can arrange to do so discreetly."

There was something comforting and stirring about having someone take care of her after a lifetime of deprivation. If Beatrice wasn't careful, she would lose her heart to Cassius.

It's only because he's been kind and considerate.

Was it though?

After Cassius had gone and she'd locked the door, Beatrice removed her hat and cloak. The ill-fitting gown sagged on her slender frame.

It didn't matter.

She'd never been one to care much about fashion—unlike her uncle, who was more fastidious and far pickier about his attire and appearance than any woman she'd ever met.

Several hoarse coughs forced their way up her throat.

Just perfect.

As if their escape weren't difficult enough, she had to become ill.

Well, Cassius would not hear a single word of complaint from her, Beatrice vowed. She would do nothing to slow down their flight.

The bed looked so inviting. To stretch out and relax would be a little slice of heaven. Sighing, she lay down, intending to rest until Cassius returned. Allowing her eyes to flutter close, she resumed her mental inventory of what she intended to do with her money.

"Beatrice!" Someone shook her shoulder. "Beatrice! Wake up."

No. I'm so tired. Just let me sleep.

"Beatrice."

The fervor in Cassius's voice finally stirred her.

Beatrice forced her leaden eyelids open.

He loomed over her, his face strained and eyes flashing.

Still half-asleep, she blinked at him groggily.

Lord, she felt positively horrid.

"I'm sorry, Cassius. I must've fallen asleep."

"'Tis of no consequence." He cast an urgent glance toward the locked door. "A man arrived fifteen minutes ago, asking about a young woman traveling with two dogs —a large boarhound and a small black mongrel."

Teddy wasn't a mongrel, though how many times had Uncle Cedric called him precisely that?

"Oh, my God." She bolted upright, her heart stampeding behind her breastbone.

Cassius speared a worried glance toward the uncovered window. Night was upon them fully now. "Thank God no one saw you enter, and the dogs are still in the coach."

"How c-could he have f-found us so fast?" She fumbled with her hair, most of which had come loose from her makeshift turban. Fingers thick and awkward, she wound her hair into a knot at the back of her head and retied the strip of lace.

"I don't know." Expression grim, he shook his head. "Since no one in the common room saw you enter, Layton and I hope he'll think he's on the wrong trail. My brother is distracting the fellow with drink and talk of soldiering. He hopes to get the chap drunk while we make our escape. He'll catch up to us on the road later on."

She slipped from the bed and pushed her feet into her slippers.

Cassius shoved her ugly hat and cloak at her. "I've already asked for a new team for the coach."

That wouldn't raise any suspicions. Leaving less than an hour after they'd arrived.

Beatrice donned both garments in a matter of seconds. However, her fingers shook so badly, she couldn't tie the bonnet's ribbons or secure the cloak's clasp.

"Here." Cassius gently pushed her quivering hands aside. "Let me do it for you."

"Thank you," she mumbled on a barely audible thread.

Terror, unlike anything she'd ever known, sent icy chills pulsating through her body, swiftly followed by a wave of heat.

Or were the flashes of cold and warmth because of her illness?

What did it matter?

Cassius finished securing her cloak, then ever-so-gently cupped her chin.

"I'll keep you safe, Beatrice. You have my word."

For her uncle to have sent a man after her this quickly didn't bode well. Beatrice would never forgive herself if something happened to Cassius while he helped her. She should never have involved him, but how else could she have escaped Brighton?

She opened her mouth to respond, but he twirled her around and gave a little shove. "Go."

FIFTEEN

The main turnpike near Stoke-on-Trent

*TWELVE HOURS AND FIVE TEAM CHANGES
LATER*

Cassius stretched his legs until his feet touched the opposite seat, then flexed his thighs. Every muscle in his body screamed for him to leap from the lumbering conveyance and stretch. God, how he despised traveling by coach, even if the company was quite exceptional.

Across from him, half turned into the seat and holding Teddy on her lap, Beatrice slept the fitful sleep of the tormented and the ill. She moved often, speaking or moaning or coughing.

Hell's clanging bells.

It hadn't occurred to him she might have contracted the same ailment that had sent her companion to bed.

A swift glance at his watch revealed the time was nearly half-past twelve.

The August sun shone high in the clear sky, unhindered by clouds.

Firming his mouth, he tried not to worry about why Layton hadn't caught up to the coach yet. An experienced soldier for over two decades, his eldest half-brother knew how to take care of himself.

Cassius arched his back and flexed his arms.

This bloody coach was far too cramped.

He asked Layton to bring an extra horse for him to ride.

Confinement in a small conveyance with Beatrice proved far too provocative and tempting. His mind kept wandering to forbidden areas, and more than once, his traitorous body had betrayed him with his growing desire for her.

He despised that weakness of his flesh.

No doubt, Beatrice would appreciate having the coach to herself, and he certainly would welcome a break from the conflicting emotions assailing him regarding her.

Lucius and Cousin Torrian had dug up more information about the Earl of Highbury and, given the implications of the evidence he'd uncovered, Father had sent

Layton to Brighton at once to dispatch the recent findings to Cassius. That was why Layton was at The Frolicking Fox Inn, a stroke of luck, to be sure.

Not only was the Earl of Highbury on the brink of bankruptcy, but he'd also reached out to known nefarious individuals of London's underworld. That disturbing information had come via Fletcher, whose contacts were vast and diverse.

What purpose Highbury had in contacting known criminals, no one knew just yet.

Cassius hadn't pieced the puzzle together, but a picture had begun to form, and it didn't bode well for Beatrice.

She would have to be told about this new revelation, of course.

But not now.

Not until she was safe and sequestered at Hefferwickshire House and was well away from Highbury's clutches. In truth, Cassius didn't think she should be told about her uncle's perfidy until she'd claimed her fortune. She would feel more in control then. Less vulnerable to her uncle's schemes and wiles.

From beneath hooded eyelids, he allowed himself the pleasure of watching her sleep. Her eyes moving behind her ivory eyelids, she breathed through her parted peach-tinted lips, snoring softly every so often.

Probably because of her cold, but her snoring was rather endearing.

What did she dream of?

A safe and secure future?

She claimed she wasn't interested in marriage, but was that due to past unpleasant experiences, her mother's unfortunate fate, or truly the desire of her heart?

Cassius didn't know her well, but from what he'd learned during their brief acquaintance and given her capacity for love and compassion toward her pets, he doubted she'd find contentment as a childless old tabby despite her protestations otherwise.

Would *he* be happy without children?

The point was moot.

He was determined to continue on the path that Providence had steered him down.

Sighing, he laid his head against the relatively clean seat back but didn't permit himself to sleep. He must remain alert. Highbury's man had found them far too easily, which confirmed Cassius's suspicions that the earl spied on his niece.

His stomach tightened at the repugnant thoughts.

Likely, the wretch had bribed someone at the coaching inn too.

Should he ever have the misfortune of meeting the Earl of Highbury again, he'd plant the blackguard a facer, that would break his perfectly straight aristocratic nose.

Not usually given to violence, Cassius shook off the unpleasant musings and directed his focus to the passing bucolic scenery.

Black-faced Shropshire sheep and white-faced, rusty-colored Hereford cattle dotted the Midland's verdant meadows and rolling hills. Occasionally, a low *moo* or bleating *baa* sounded in the distance. A pair of turtle doves took to wing as the coach lumbered past. The distinctive *whir, whir* of their flight, only enhanced the early afternoon's tranquility.

Beatrice murmured something in her sleep, and he caressed her face with his gaze.

It was the only caress Cassius would ever give her.

She wasn't his obligation, but how could he leave her to Highbury's evil designs?

Cassius considered himself a godly man who tried to do what was right. He wasn't perfect by any means, but who was?

To abandon her was unthinkable. Unpardonable. Unconscionable.

Many men would have done so without a qualm.

The truth of it was, he could never forgive himself.

Regardless, once they arrived at the Latham ducal estate, he meant to turn her over to his parents' care and wash his hands of her. Mother liked nothing better than coming to some unfortunate soul's rescue. Father would use his considerable influence to ensure Beatrice not only claimed her inheritance, but Highbury left her alone.

Cassius's major regret in passing Beatrice's care to his parents was he would not finish her portrait.

Keep telling yourself that lie, and you might just come to believe it.

Nevertheless, nothing could compel him to risk his heart again, and the more time he spent with Beatrice Fairfax, the greater that possibility became. In the last few days, there'd been too many moments with her, where something tried to take root and sprout into an emotion beyond sympathy and compassion.

He curled his hands into fists.

By God, he could not allow that.

No, he would not open himself to that kind of pain and suffering ever again.

Beatrice is not Constanza.

He shoved the unwelcome thought aside.

It didn't matter.

Besides, hadn't he already done far more for Beatrice than most people would have done?

Indeed, Cassius had.

He owed her nothing else.

Given this unexpected interruption to his painting schedule, he'd likely not have enough paintings completed for the exhibition.

He accepted the situation for what it was rather than become vexed or disappointed.

There would be other shows.

And it wasn't as if he'd hung his career on the British Institution's art show.

"You look rather serious." Beatrice's sleep-husky voice drew Cassius's attention back inside the conveyance. Or had her cold made her voice hoarse?

Her drowsy hazel eyes reminded him of a sleepy kitten.

She coughed into her handkerchief, her narrow shoulders shaking.

Teddy yawned and blinked his one good eye.

"I'm a good listener if you care to talk about whatever is troubling you, Cassius."

She was troubling him, but he could hardly tell her that, now, could he?

Instead, he produced a flippant grin.

"You snore, Beatrice."

Rather than become affronted, she raised a reddish-blonde eyebrow and gave an arch look, humor twinkling in her eyes.

"A gallant gentleman would never say so," she said without a hint of her stutter.

He couldn't control his shout of laughter, which caused both dogs to cock their heads and thump their tails. "Are you suggesting I'm not chivalrous?"

"Oh, my heavens, not at all." At once, Beatrice pressed a hand to her chest, and her expression grew contrite. "Forgive me. You have more than proven your chivalry, Cassius. Please know, I meant no offense."

"I'm not offended, Beatrice. I was but teasing."

Leaning forward, he took her hand in his and gave her fingers a light squeeze. A lifetime of abuse at Highbury's hands likely caused her unnecessary contrition. "You mustn't take everything to heart."

She raised her focus from her hand cradled in his, and their gazes locked.

Just like an enchanted moment from a fairytale, time stood still—suspended in a magical haze. He couldn't have torn his gaze from hers if a score of armed highwaymen had descended upon the coach.

Her rosebud mouth parted, and emotion softened the corners of her eyes.

Stop this insanity!

Do not encourage her feelings or give her false hope.

Dropping her hand a trifle rougher than was necessary, Cassius reclined against the seat once more.

You're an unconscionable cad, Cassius Nathan Everett Westbrook.

SIXTEEN

A couple of miles past the turnpike

Confusion and hurt whisked across Beatrice's face before she arranged her features into an unreadable mien. He'd witnessed her doing that very thing when her uncle chastised her harshly. Nevertheless, her eyes spoke volumes as she peeked at him from beneath those gold-tipped lashes.

He recognized that look of yearning.

Bloody, sodding hell.

Her regard was anything but impartial, and he almost cursed aloud.

Where the devil was Layton?

Much more of this, and Cassius would climb up on the driver's seat and squeeze between the coachmen. Or—

God help them both—haul Beatrice into his arms and kiss her senseless.

Which would create a whole other conundrum he didn't want to deal with.

"The shade is pleasant, is it not?"

So she'd resorted to small talk to ease the tension between them, so thick a sword couldn't cleave it in two.

The trees lining this section of the turnpike provided a pleasant reprieve from what looked to be an unseasonably hot day. Still, sweat beaded Cassius's upper lip. "Aye."

In the distance, hoofbeats sounded, carrying through the lowered coach windows on the peaceful summer day.

Cassius poked his head out of the opening.

Layton.

At last.

And thank God, for had it been the man hunting Beatrice, things would have swiftly become ugly.

Cassius knocked on the roof.

One of the coachmen slid the small window open at the coach's front. "Aye, gov?"

"Please stop. My brother approaches."

"Aye, gov."

Cassius gestured toward the door.

"Would you care to stretch your legs, Beatrice? The dogs too?"

"Oh, yes." A brilliant smile lit her face, and he was

hard-pressed not to blink like a besotted fool. "I'm sure Nala and Teddy need to relieve themselves."

After helping her alight, Cassius leaned against the coach's side, surreptitiously observing her walk with her dogs.

She spoke to them in a soft undertone between brief bouts of coughing. Both promptly relieved themselves, and chagrin knocked at his ribs.

So intent had he been in outrunning the chap hired to find her, he'd spared little time for the dogs' needs.

A couple of minutes later, riding atop a bay gelding and leading a sorrel mare and a gray gelding with a black mane, Layton drew up beside the conveyance.

Beatrice eyed the extra horses with a beleaguered expression.

Cassius crossed to his brother and took hold of the reins of the other two horses while Layton dismounted.

Layton grinned. His good eye, not covered by a black patch, twinkled with humor as the dogs greeted him with cautious canine sniffs but no barking.

"Hello, there." He glanced at Cassius. "Who do we have here?"

"The boarhound is Nala, and the little chap is Teddy," Cassius said.

Layton scratched Nala behind the ears, then crouched and did the same with Teddy.

"Ah, the mite is also blind in one eye." He ruffled

the fur on Teddy's back before standing upright. "I think we shall be the greatest of comrades, my little friend."

"You're later than I expected." Cassius speared a harried look down the road.

Nothing stirred up dust in the distance.

That was a good sign.

"Yes, well." Layton sent Beatrice a guarded glance as he leaned toward Cassius and said in a low tone, "Things didn't go *quite* as we planned."

Cassius angled his head, careful to keep his escalating alarm from showing. "How so?"

Layton slapped the dust from his buff-colored trousers. "The chap's three friends arrived after you departed. Evidently, they'd taken different routes to determine which path you traveled on. A barmaid spotted you leaving with Miss Fairfax." He arched a mocking eyebrow. "The wench had no qualms about sharing that snippet for the right price."

Bollocks.

Highbury must, indeed, be desperate to retrieve Beatrice. But how did the earl think to gain control of her fortune?

Certainly not through legal means.

"How did you manage to evade them and leave without them following you?" A very real worry because Cassius and Layton would be hard-pressed to defend

Beatrice against four, possibly more hired thugs, even if Layton carried a gun.

Layton slid Beatrice another cautious glance.

"Let's just say another barmaid took a fancy to me— said I looked like a swashbuckler." He grinned, a devilish glint in his gray eye when he winked. "At my request, she produced laudanum, and I dosed the blokes' tankards with enough to take down a draft horse. I doubt they've awoken yet."

Cassius chose not to inquire further from his eldest brother about the details of his delay. It didn't take a great deal of imagination to work those out, and he'd spare Beatrice's tender sensibilities.

Beatrice cleared her throat, then darted her tongue out to dampen her lower lip, betraying her nervousness. She approached them.

"Forgive me for interrupting, but did I hear you correctly, Captain Westbrook? My uncle sent more than one man after me?"

"Forgive me, Beatrice." Cassius wasn't usually a clod-pole when it came to manners, but this wasn't exactly a Grosvenor Square drawing room either.

"Layton, allow me to introduce Miss Beatrice Fairfax. Beatrice, my brother, Captain Layton Westbrook."

"At your service, Miss Fairfax." Layton bowed. "And yes. I encountered four men last night. I don't believe that is all of them, either." He swept his hand toward the horses. "Hence the need for us to ride the rest of the way to Hefferwickshire House."

Beatrice shook her head, panic darkening her eyes to jade. "B-but I do not ride."

Cassius read the concern on Layton's face.

There was no need for him to voice the danger they were all in.

"You'll ride before me, Beatrice." Though it would likely kill Cassius to have her bum bouncing on his nether regions for hours on end. He almost groaned aloud at the thought, but the smug glint in Layton's eye kept him silent.

Her color high, she shook her head, causing her bonnet ribbons to flap with the vehement motion. "No... I—"

"You do not have a choice." Cassius cut her off, his tone not permitting any argument. "It is one thing to endanger myself. I shan't endanger my brother or you."

She snapped her mouth shut, but her eyes berated him.

Yet she must know he spoke the truth.

She didn't have a choice.

With the horses, they could cut through fields and take shortcuts a coach could not manage.

Layton removed his dusty bicorn hat and swiped a gloved hand across his forehead.

"I'll take care of the coachmen. A hefty bribe will

encourage them to take a turnpike in the opposite direction." He eyed the coach. "Luggage?"

"None." Thank God for that small favor. "But there is food, a blanket, and a canteen inside the coach. We'll need those."

Layton grunted and nodded before retrieving the items and then approaching the curious drivers and murmuring to them beneath his breath.

Eyes wide and worried, Beatrice nervously licked her lips again.

Cassius narrowed his eyes.

She looked feverish.

Was she up to the hard trek ahead?

She must be.

The sorrel mare snorted and tossed her head.

"I've never even sat on a horse, Cassius," Beatrice murmured, eyeing the horses with undisguised dismay.

Sighing, he placed his hands on her shoulders. She was delicate, but not frail.

She didn't feel overly hot either.

"I promised to keep you safe, Beatrice." He searched her vulnerable face. "Do you trust me?"

She was silent for a long moment, then gave a single nod. "Yes."

Layton returned to their side just as the coach rumbled away.

Cassius vaulted onto the bay gelding, then gave his brother a nod.

Before she could protest, Layton grasped her by the waist and lifted her into Cassius's waiting arms.

He plopped her sideways atop his thighs, effectively silencing her little shriek of terror.

She promptly wrapped her arms around his waist, clinging to him as tightly as a barnacle to a ship.

Layton secured the food and other items to the riderless horse. "We can rotate horses. That should allow us to ride longer."

Cassius nodded.

Teddy pranced in circles, looking up at Beatrice, his little brown eye filled with worry.

"I'll carry the small dog." Layton climbed into the saddle, Teddy under one arm. "The large one can run beside us."

After an anxious glance at his mistress, Teddy circled two times and lay down.

"Traitor," Beatrice mumbled into Cassius's chest.

She trembled against him like a leaf, buffeted by a springtime gale. Her essence of soap and lavender wafted upward.

God help him.

Beatrice Fairfax was every bit as intoxicating as the finest brandy.

"Hold on, Beatrice. We ride."

SEVENTEEN

The South Pennines
Approximately fifty miles from Cumberland

NEAR MIDNIGHT THAT EVENING

I *cannot endure this much longer.*

But Beatrice would.

For as long as it took.

Even if each step the tired horse took sent a jolt of pain up her spine. Even if her lungs burned with each indrawn breath. And even if she felt as weak as a newborn kitten.

At long last, the weary horses drew to a halt before a hunting lodge. At least that's what Beatrice thought it was in the shadowy light. To the left of the ramshackle building, a lean-to stood at a haphazard angle. That must be for horses.

She gravitated her attention back to the dilapidated building. Actually, it wasn't in as appalling shape as she'd first thought, but if anyone had used the shelter in the past decade, she'd dance a jig. Still, she didn't want to consider what creepy-crawly creatures might have taken up residence in the neglected structure.

Nala promptly plopped to the ground and rested her head on her front paws. The poor dog was unused to walking for so many hours, and tomorrow wouldn't be much kinder to her, though Cassius assured Beatrice they should reach the ducal estate by mid-afternoon.

Beatrice worried the dog's paws would become tender and raw, but what else were they to do?

She would never leave Nala behind, and there was simply no way to carry her.

Beatrice swallowed back a haze of tears.

Not given to weepiness, she credited the waterworks to exhaustion, fear, feeling sorer than she'd ever been in her life, and being sick without so much as an herbal tea to ease her tormented throat. How she would survive another bone-jarring, muscle-tormenting day atop a horse, she didn't allow herself to contemplate.

It had only taken a couple of hours for her to mostly overcome her fear of toppling off and to admit that riding did indeed enable them to travel tracks and trails they would never have managed by coach.

So far, they'd evaded Uncle Cedric's henchmen, but Beatrice credited that with Captain Westbrook's keen intelligence and stealth. Had she and Cassius not come upon him, this venture might very well have had a vastly different outcome.

Gritting her teeth against the pulsing ache in her spine from sitting at the awkward angle for hours on end, Beatrice lifted her weary gaze and took in the small glen. Water burbled, annoyingly cheerfully from somewhere beyond the cabin.

In another time and place, she might've appreciated the landscapes they'd passed through today, and even this ethereal scenery where a fairy or a wood nymph might peek at them from behind a Bracken or Lady Fern.

However, the ferocity with which her uncle chased her loomed, stealing any excitement or enjoyment she might've otherwise had regarding her first journey away from Brighton.

An owl hooted, *twit-twoo, twit-twoo*, the call lonely and haunting in the breezeless night.

Though she didn't give a moment's credence to the silly folklore of hearing an owl's hoot foretelling misfortune or death, nevertheless, a shudder rippled up her back, and she pulled her cloak tighter around her.

She'd vacillated between freezing cold and scorching hot for the better part of three hours now. Perspiration dampened her gown along her spine, under her arms, and between her breasts.

What she wouldn't give for that bath she'd missed last night.

Not only had she never been this miserably tired, she'd never been so dirty, and she suspected she smelled of sweat.

She took a dainty sniff and curled her nose.

A few miles back, Cassius had murmured into her ear that they had reached The South Pennines. His sturdy arms around her throughout the harrowing journey had not only supported her but comforted her as well. She refused to let her mind wander to the intimacy of sitting on his lap and the forbidden feelings that closeness stirred in her.

The higher elevation brought cooler temperatures, especially as the night wore on. Moonlight filtered through the leaves of the woodland canopy overhead, dappling the ground with silvery light.

Captain Westbrook dismounted with the ease of someone accustomed to long hours in the saddle. After placing Teddy on the ground, who promptly trotted to Nala and touched noses with her, the captain stretched his arms wide.

"Ready to dismount, Miss Fairfax?" he asked.

She nodded, then realized he might not be able to see her in the muted half-light. "Yes."

He lifted Beatrice to the ground, and she almost crumpled, so stiff were her legs. A small moan filtered past her lips.

Oh, God.

Never had she felt this wretched.

"I have you." Sympathy tempered the captain's voice. "Give your legs a few minutes to adjust to your weight."

"When I get my inheritance, I'm purchasing the most luxurious coach money can buy. I'll even pay for extra padding on the seats, which shall fold out into a comfortable bed." She wouldn't, of course. To do so would be an unnecessary and flamboyant waste of funds.

Cassius and his brother chuckled.

Brutes.

"Can you stand on your own now?" Captain Westbrook asked as Cassius slid from his horse.

She gave a stiff nod.

Stand?

Yes.

Move?

Beatrice wasn't positive she could. Not without help.

It bruised her pride to be so needy when the brothers had ridden just as long as she and seemed no worse the wear from the journey.

"I'll see to the horses, Cassius." The captain gathered the reins. "Why don't you help Miss Fairfax inside and see if there's a candle or lamp?"

A bed? A washstand? A fire?

As if reading her mind, Cassius murmured, "We don't dare light a fire, though."

Rot and bother.

She tried to hide her shivering, but Cassius noticed.

"Bring the horse blankets in," he said to his brother. "At least we'll have those for warmth tonight."

Wonderful.

Beatrice could add sweaty horse to the list of other odors she already smelled on herself. What a lovely way to meet the Duke and Duchess of Latham. Disheveled. Stinking. Sick. And pursued by ruffians. Surely, she would make a grand impression.

As she skimmed the ramshackle hut with her dubious regard, another shudder shook her, but it wasn't caused by cold this time.

In truth, she wasn't altogether keen on being the first to enter the cottage, which likely was the home to a hoard of spiders and four-legged creatures with beady eyes, twitchy whiskers, and sharp teeth. Nevertheless, she'd been a tremendous burden to these two men already, and she'd bite off her tongue before voicing any of her fears.

A cough shook her shoulders and battered her ribs, but she muffled the sound by covering her mouth with a handkerchief. So help her God, she would not be the cause of them getting caught. She didn't think her uncle's men knew the shortcuts or back trails they'd taken to reach this woodland.

She prayed they didn't.

In flat places where the horses' hooves left imprints, the captain had secured a bushy branch to the third horse to drag along the ground and sweep away the signs that they'd passed by. The trick wouldn't fool a trained tracker, but Beatrice doubted her uncle had hired the men chasing her for that particular skill.

"Let me help you." Cassius took her elbow and allowed her to set a slow pace toward the lodge.

To her surprise, once she forced the stiff muscles to work, the soreness eased, though she still toddled along like an ancient crone.

A giggle escaped her, followed by a hacking cough.

Forehead puzzled, Cassius looked downward. "What's so funny?"

"I'm walking like an old lady." She wavered, and he quickly steadied her.

"Cassius?"

He bent near, concern pleating the corners of his face.

"I'm sorry to be a burden." Black spots danced before her vision, and the buzzing in her ears grew louder.

She closed her eyes but forced them back open.

The cottage was too far away.

Beatrice couldn't do it.

She didn't have one ounce of strength left.

As if sensing her dilemma, Cassius scooped her into his powerful arms.

"Thank—"

Then everything went blank.

EIGHTEEN

NEAR DAWN THE FOLLOWING MORNING

One hand planted on his hip and the other cupping his nape, Cassius stood beside the improvised bed that Beatrice lay upon, four feet from the sooty hearth. Concern tightened his throat and worry made him press his mouth into a severe line.

If he didn't fear discovery, and if the grimy chimney weren't in such poor condition, he would have risked a fire, just for the much-needed light.

Beatrice hadn't stirred after fainting.

Not even when he'd settled her on the two horse blankets Layton had hurriedly laid upon the wooden floor, untied her cloak, unbuttoned the top five buttons of her gown, and removed her stockings and shoes.

Both dogs lay next to her, their worried gazes trained on her wan face. Every few minutes, Teddy whimpered and looked to Cassius or Layton, asking them to help his mistress.

Cassius shared the dogs' dismay.

Beatrice burned with fever and, other than wiping her with cool water from the stream behind the cabin, there was naught he could do. He glanced to the side to where his brother leaned against the stone hearth, arms folded, a look of consternation creasing his expression.

"She's too weak to travel on horseback, Layton."

Layton nodded but remained silent.

Cassius closed his eyes.

They could contrive some sort of litter to drag behind a horse, but that would slow them down and possibly make them sitting ducks for Highbury's thugs.

If Beatrice had contracted the same illness as Millborn, she might worsen even more. His gut told him she needed medical attention, and she sure as blazes couldn't get it in a run-down cabin in the woods.

Facing his brother, Cassius sighed. "You'll have to go for help."

"Aye." Layton gave a solemn nod.

There was nothing else to do.

Cassius would remain here and care for Beatrice as best he could.

If Layton rode hard and nothing unforeseen caused a delay, he could arrive at Hefferwickshire by mid-morning. It might take an hour or two to get a coach ready, reach a physician, and round up men to accompany him back to the woods.

The return trip to this God-forsaken glen would be slower, but if all went well, *and* if the Good Lord smiled down upon them, help could be here by late tonight.

"I'll leave now." Layton straightened. "I'll try to hurry."

Cassius nodded, taking in their primitive surroundings.

The lone candle he'd located last night wouldn't last more than an hour or two. Thank God Beatrice wasn't aware of the spiderwebs, scampering little feet, or the bat that had darted around the small enclosure until Layton had shooed the terrified creature out the open door.

Layton crossed the room and grasped Cassius's shoulder. "I don't know what Miss Fairfax means to you, and it's none of my business, little brother. But you plainly care for her, or you would never have agreed to this madcap scheme."

Madcap, indeed.

"It doesn't matter." Cassius shook his head. "As soon

as I've delivered Beatrice Fairfax to Hefferwickshire House, I'm washing my hands of the responsibility. You know I vowed to never become emotionally entangled again."

Beatrice moaned and tossed her head back and forth before quieting.

"I know, and I understand." Layton well should after Virginia had left him for another officer and tried to kill him to boot.

A few years back, he'd spoken of adopting a child but hadn't mentioned it again, so perhaps he intended to live out his life alone, as did Cassius.

Layton tilted his head toward Beatrice. "But does *she* know that?"

Something that resembled a wry smile tried to wrestle Cassius's mouth upward.

"Beatrice has informed me, quite succinctly, that she no more desires to marry than you or I do. I believe it has something to do with her illegitimacy, but she's never said as much to me."

"Interesting," Layton said, his tone suspiciously neutral.

What did that mean?

Cassius narrowed his eyes. He needed to be more careful in the future. His brother already believed he harbored feelings toward Beatrice—something he hadn't even admitted to himself.

Layton aimed his too-astute gaze toward their patient.

Perspiration dotted her pale face.

"I'll leave my gun and ammunition." He pulled a wicked-looking knife from his waistband and laid it on a rickety table that appeared as if it might collapse at any moment. "My knife too."

Shaking his head, Cassius tried to hand the blade back.

"You'll need something to protect yourself, Layton."

Grinning, Layton backed away, his hands held up, palms outward. "I'm the soldier, remember? *I* know how to defend myself. *You're* an artist."

Cassius didn't take offense at his brother's unintended insult.

Layton gave the pistol a doubtful glance. "When was the last time you fired a gun?"

"Don't worry about me." Cassius lifted the Manton pistol, testing the weight in his hand. "I'm fully capable of discharging a firearm if necessary."

Pray to God it does not come to that.

Layton turned his attention to Beatrice once more. "I'd strip her of that gown and wipe her limbs and face with cool water. Try to get her to drink a bit of water too."

"I shall." They'd found a bucket outside that wasn't completely rusted out.

It was a good thing Beatrice wasn't awake to comprehend her vulnerable state or how completely and utterly compromised she'd become. Only her fortune provided her a jot of leverage, because once word spread of her disgrace, as it surely would, Society would shun her.

Except for his family.

They would be there for her.

He suppressed a grimace.

It wasn't fair of him to burden Mother and Father with Beatrice.

"I'd best not delay." Layton pulled him in for a brief, but powerful hug. "If all goes well, look for us sometime late this evening."

Neither of them mentioned what must be on both their minds... *What would happen if the earl's thugs discovered Beatrice and Cassius before Layton returned?*

"Cassius, if I don't come back, travel north, keeping the sun on your left. You'll eventually come to a main track."

Cassius gripped his brother's arm. "You'll be back."

Layton took his leave, taking a second horse with him to throw any trackers off his trail. It wasn't as if Cassius could have bundled Beatrice onto a saddle in any event, but it brought home just how vulnerable they were.

Head cocked, Cassius stood just outside the hunting lodge, listening long after the hoofbeats faded away. The warbles and songs of various birds who called the woodlands home and the wind gently rustling the silver birch and oak leaves enhanced the natural serenity.

Which is exactly what he hoped to hear.

If anyone approached, the birds falling silent and the red squirrels' *kuk-kuk-kuk* would sound the alarm.

Layton had already opened the shutters covering the cottage's two windows, but for good measure, Cassius propped the door open with a rock. He'd be damned if he'd sit inside with the windows covered and the door bolted like a convict in an underground cell.

Sighing, he retreated inside and directed his attention to Beatrice.

Even though she couldn't hear him, he spoke to her.

"I have to remove your gown, Beatrice, but I'll leave your shift on."

He kneeled at her side and laid the back of his hand against her fevered forehead. She burned with the illness that assailed her.

"You have a fever, and I must try to get your temperature down." In his many musings about Beatrice, Cassius never dreamed he'd play nursemaid to this beautiful woman. "I promise I shan't look upon you any more than absolutely necessary."

As he set to unfastening the gown's remaining buttons, he explained what he intended. "I'll wipe you with a cool cloth when I've finished. It should help make you more comfortable."

Nala lifted her head, staring at him with soulful eyes before once more resting her muzzle on her great paws. She heaved a forlorn sigh.

Cassius paused in his ministrations of Beatrice to run a hand down the boarhound's back and to scratch behind Teddy's ears.

"I know you're worried." He slid Beatrice a sidelong glance, drawing his eyebrows together in disquiet. "I am too."

Shouldn't she have roused by now?

It was hard to know if she was deeply asleep, her body fighting whatever sickness afflicted her, or if she was unconscious.

As he slid the gown down her hips and past her shapely legs, he forbade the artist in him to stare in appreciation at her well-shaped thighs and calves, strong and supple from daily walks, no doubt. After all, he'd just promised her he wouldn't ogle her.

Stirring slightly, she moaned softly before a harsh cough shook her.

Worry clawing at his ribs, Cassius tossed the gown onto the table before hastily dipping a cloth in the bucket of cool water. After wringing the rag out, he gently ran the damp cloth over her face, neck, and shoulders, and then down her legs.

"Beatrice? Can you hear me?"

She didn't respond, but her chest rose and fell in a steady rhythm.

He glanced at Nala, and an idea took root. He pointed to the door. "Guard."

To his immense satisfaction, the large hound promptly rose and walked to the entrance where she lay across the threshold, facing outward, ever vigilant. Not only could she hear far better than he could, but dogs' sense of smell was vastly superior to humans.

The remaining horse snorted, the sound filtering inside the small structure as a few valiant rays of sun poked through the overhead canopy and timidly ventured inside through the open window casings.

After soaking the cloth in the little remaining water in the bucket, Cassius wrung it out and laid it tenderly across Beatrice's forehead. He rose, clasping the bucket as he did.

Teddy stood, wagging his tail as he looked between Cassius and Beatrice.

"Don't worry, little fellow. I'm just fetching more water."

He needed to feed the dogs too, but they were down to a few pieces of bread, a hunk of cheese, and two apples. Not exactly a feast.

If Beatrice wasn't so ill, he might try to set a snare or catch fish, but he dared not leave her alone for any length of time.

He tucked Layton's knife into his belt. In these circumstances, wisdom decreed caution.

Nala sat up as he approached the door.

Cassius stepped through and then turned back. "Guard."

At once, she resumed her diligent stance.

The stream was but a few dozen footsteps from the cottage. Once he'd filled the bucket as much as he could before it seeped from the sides, he glanced around and couldn't contain his jubilant grin.

Stinging nettle and blackberries.

In the dusky dawn, he'd missed the plants.

Grandmama was an expert on herbs, and over the years, she'd shared her knowledge with her grandchildren, though none had the keen interest in natural medicines that their paternal grandmother had.

Nevertheless, Cassius remembered his lessons and knew that stinging nettle could help Beatrice, although he preferred using dried leaves for tea.

Still, beggars couldn't be choosers.

He'd need to retrieve his gloves from the hut and find something to put the leaves in, however, because touching them barehanded would leave his hands raw and itching.

He meant to gather ripe blackberries too. It wasn't much in the way of food, but it was something.

Though he'd have to risk a brief fire to heat water for the tea, he felt more hopeful than he had an hour ago. Lengthening his strides, he hurried to the cottage. As he rounded the corner of the cabin, alarm raised his nape hair.

Nala no longer guarded the doorway.

He broke into a run, sloshing water over the bucket rim in his haste.

A couple of feet beyond the threshold, he slid to a stop.

Beatrice, her brilliant sunset-streaked curtain of hair framing her slender shoulders, sat on her knees in her filmy shift, her faithful dogs on either side of her.

Confusion and fear creased her still waxen face, and upon spying him, tears pooled in her magnificent, but lucid, hazel eyes.

"I woke up and n-no one was here," she whispered brokenly, her voice a harsh rasp. "I th-thought you'd left me."

Cassius's heart lurched and swelled behind his ribs. He clenched his hands, fighting the overwhelming desire to race across the tiny cottage and gather her into his arms. To assure her that he would never leave her.

But he would.

He must.

Mustn't he?

Bollocks and blisters.

He was on the verge of toppling into the abyss he'd struggled so hard to protect himself from.

"Layton went for help," he said. "You are too sick to travel on horseback, so I stayed here with you."

He lowered the bucket to the floor, and slowly, as if she were a frightened wild animal, approached her.

Lower lip quivering, she peered up at him.

Proud and vulnerable.

Hopeful but hesitant.

"I promised I would protect you, Beatrice. I honor my word."

It had become more than that. Much, much more, though what and when, Cassius couldn't say for certain.

He dropped to one knee beside her, and she flung herself into his arms. "I was so afraid."

How well he knew what that admission cost this independent woman.

Reeling with emotion, Cassius wrapped his arms around her quaking form, whispering soothing words into her silky hair.

If he hadn't already given her his heart, it would have leaped from his chest to lie at her feet.

I'm lost. Utterly and irreversibly lost.

Regardless, Beatrice would never know.

Because he'd taken an oath to never love again, and his word was his bond.

NINETEEN

Still in The South Pennines hunting lodge

EVENING THAT SAME DAY

Sitting on the horse blankets and propped up against the fireplace hearth, Beatrice sipped her fourth cup of tepid stinging nettle tea and tried not to notice the plump spider perched on a corner web. She couldn't say she enjoyed the earthy, grassy taste, but the brew contained a faint, unexpected sweetness, making it slightly more palatable.

The tea seemed to help her symptoms too.

Cassius had extinguished the tiny fire immediately after heating water for her tea, explaining they couldn't risk someone seeing the smoke.

Throughout the day, she'd gradually improved to the point she'd finally convinced Cassius that she would not cock up her toes any minute. Frowning in disapproval, he'd allowed her to sit up and don her borrowed gown, though her bare toes peeked at her from beneath the hem.

Her stomach growled, but she tried to ignore the gnawing hunger.

They had no food left.

He'd given each dog a piece of bread and a handful of blackberries.

Teddy and Nala gobbled the small fare as if starving, and Beatrice's heart ached for them. Both had known deprivation before, and she had promised they never would again. She'd failed them in that regard.

If Cassius hadn't watched her like a hawk, she would've sneaked her piece of bread, slice of cheese, and handful of blackberries to the dogs, but he'd made certain she'd eaten every crumb and every juicy berry. She was grateful, for the small meal had fortified her, and though far from well, she felt markedly better. Enough to experience chagrin for hurling herself into his arms, wearing nothing but a thin, cotton shift.

Teddy's tummy growled and guilt pierced her.

She ought to have considered what her flight from Brighton would cost her beloved pets. Had she planned better, they might not be in these dire circumstances. But how could she have planned something that came about on the spur of the moment? And how could she have predicted she'd fall ill?

Beatrice's ruminating brought her train of thought to her other pets. She had every confidence that Hans would care for them. Still, Uncle Cedric might question the lad. Of course, Hans knew nothing, but Uncle Cedric could be unpredictable.

She shifted, laying her left ankle across her right. Though she'd folded the blankets into quarters, the floor proved uncomfortable.

Cassius stood at the entrance, one arm raised and resting against the rough wood frame. Exhaustion fairly radiated from him, detectable in his slightly slumped shoulders and bowed neck.

He's exhausted because of me.

To Beatrice's knowledge, he hadn't slept for more than a few minutes at a time since they hightailed it from Brighton. How he stayed awake, let alone stood, was beyond her.

Remorse castigated her.

She'd put him in danger, much more so with her inability to travel.

With his back to her, Beatrice studied Cassius as she examined the feelings, trying to take root in her heart. Sentiments she couldn't allow to grow and flourish.

Heat swept her cheeks, and the warmth wasn't from her fever returning.

She'd practically climbed into his lap that morning.

A songbird trilled outside. She did not know what type it might be, but the sound blended perfectly with the evening's tranquility.

God, she'd been terrified when she'd woken and found herself alone, petrified that the Westbrook brothers had left her in these mountains. She could no more find her way to civilization than a crawling infant could.

She ought to have known Cassius wouldn't abandon her, and her only excuse was that her illness-befuddled mind had made it hard to think logically.

This morning, he had held her for several long minutes as she'd sobbed into his shoulder, drenching his shirt until her panic subsided. He smelled of soap, starch, cedarwood, and a pleasant musky aroma that was his unique scent.

He'd removed his neckcloth and unbuttoned the top of his shirt.

His rolled-up shirtsleeves exposed raven black hair on his forearms and peeked from the tantalizing vee below his collarbone. Something she ought not to have noticed in her distressed state and which she refused to contemplate when she'd recovered her equanimity.

When her fit of weeping had ended, he'd set her on the blankets and handed her a cool, damp cloth to erase the evidence of her tears.

Experience had taught her that her eyes would remain swollen and red for an hour or two.

She must've looked a sight.

As soon as she'd composed herself, Cassius had retreated behind his wall of cool politesse again—had once more erected that fortified wall he used as a buttress from getting too close to her. From letting her get too close to him as well.

She recognized the pattern by now.

It should not bother her.

Should it?

After all, she wasn't interested in their relationship developing into something more, either.

Liar. You don't really believe that.

No, Beatrice would not—could not—entertain dangerous, foolish ideas. Without compunction, she shoved the traitorous thoughts over the edge of a very steep mental cliff.

If she hadn't decided many years ago that she would never trust a man to the point of loving him and giving him her heart, Cassius Westbrook might be the very gentleman who could have convinced her that love and the potential for happiness were worth the risk of heartbreak. But she had made that decision, and she would not regret her choices.

As much as she trusted him, she couldn't extend that confidence to her heart.

Look what had happened to Mama.

She'd loved a man who had deceived her into giving herself to him with the promise of marriage when the bounder was already married. Mama had learned the truth too late—when she already carried Beatrice in her belly.

Oh, the scathing scorn and disparaging contempt Mama had endured.

Even as a young child, Beatrice remembered the snubs, the elevated noses, and turned backs. As if Mama were diseased. Those hypocritical snobs.

Uncle Cedric had only reinforced Beatrice's perception of men as self-centered, thoughtless, and inconsiderate creatures.

Cassius Westbrook might be the exception to the rule, but Beatrice would not gamble her future on that. Besides, after his broken betrothal, he had locked his heart and thrown away the key.

Moreover, in her half-unconscious, half-awake state, at some point, she'd heard Cassius telling his brother he couldn't wait to reach their family home so he could wash his hands of her.

Not in so many words, but she'd caught the gist of what he meant.

He didn't want to love anyone either.

Hadn't he been more than clear on that front?

It was far wiser and safer not to risk one's heart.

Fortunately, unlike most women who depended

utterly on men, Beatrice possessed independent wealth and need never submit to a man's dictates again. Well, once she collected her inheritance in London, that would be the case. Until then, she was wholly reliant upon Cassius.

All day, she'd strained to hear the slightest unnatural sound in the woodlands. Anything to alert her to an unwanted human presence. Instead, bird calls filtered through the trees, and squirrels chattered back and forth. The hours crawled by with the slowness of a snail on hot pavement until her nerves were bowstring tense with anticipation.

Though Cassius affected an air of nonchalance, he didn't fool her.

His keen artist's eyes missed nothing.

If a dog twitched an ear or lifted a snout and sniffed the air, his shoulders tensed and his features hardened.

Idly petting Teddy, Beatrice swung her attention to the open window to her right. It was impossible to tell the precise time, but from the gradual quieting of the woodlands and waning light, she guessed it must be nigh on to dusk.

She coughed, not the lung-rattling hack of twenty-four hours ago, but a productive cough.

Cassius glanced over his shoulder, concern pleating his handsome face.

It was his nature to care about others.

Too bad that Italian woman had wounded him so badly. He'd have made someone—not Beatrice, of course —a wonderful husband. With his patience and compassion, he would have been an exceptional father too.

"You needn't fret. I'm feeling much improved, Cassius." She offered what she hoped was a reassuring smile. It also didn't escape her how little she stuttered when she spoke to him. "I'm certain I don't have the same illness afflicting Millborn."

Or perhaps, being in excellent health otherwise, unlike Millborn, Beatrice's body had fought the sickness.

Giving a brief nod, Cassius tightened the firm line of his mouth. "Nevertheless, you probably should lie down and rest. You've been up for a couple of hours now. It will be dark soon, and the journey to my father's estate shall test your fortitude, even in a coach."

So Beatrice had guessed right about the time.

"You should rest too, Cassius. I know you are completely done in."

The truth was, she would welcome his company nearby. Something small rustled around beneath the floorboards, and she swore she'd seen tiny beady eyes peeking at her from a gap between the wall planks.

Though she put on a brave front, sleeping in the pitch dark without a fire to dispel the darkness unsettled her— never mind the spiders, creepy crawlers, and rodents. Several times during her childhood, Uncle Cedric had locked her in her bedchamber with no light as punishment for some imagined infraction.

Nonetheless, Beatrice would bite off her tongue before breathing a word of her fear of the dark to Cassius.

He needed no more burdens. She'd saddled him with too many already.

Besides, he'd said his brother and others should be there by late evening. She could bear a few hours in the dark with Nala and Teddy close at hand. Especially if Cassius was there too.

"When do you think Captain Westbrook and the others will arrive?" Beatrice tried to sound casual as she set aside the empty, dented tin cup missing its handle.

Tilting his head upward, Cassius appeared to be studying the sky, although what he could see through the dense overgrowth, she wasn't certain.

At last, he shrugged. "I'm not certain. If there are no complications, before midnight, I should think."

Four or five hours?

That wasn't so long.

He approached her. "Do you need privacy outside before we settle in?"

Beatrice did, and she very much doubted either of them would sleep a wink.

"Please." She nodded and gave him a grateful smile as he helped her stand.

Her legs no longer felt like rubber, though the muscles still protested any movement.

Wrapping an arm around her waist, Cassius steadied her and led her behind the hunting lodge. She rather liked his muscular arm supporting her, but she refused to lean into his strength. It wouldn't do to become too accustomed to his support or protection.

In a few days, they'd part ways, and she'd probably never see him again.

A powerful wave of sadness swept over her.

Naturally, Nala and Teddy followed them outdoors. Assured that Beatrice was safe, the dogs began nosing around to take care of their business too.

"I'll be nearby if you need me. Just call." Cassius released her and disappeared.

This business of relieving herself outdoors was a whole new experience for Beatrice and one she was grateful was for a limited duration. She made a mental note to ensure that during her travels, accommodations for personal needs would always be available. This rustic lifestyle might appeal to some women, but she was not among them.

For the first time in her life, she realized she might just be a bit snobbish after all.

After finishing, she took a deep breath and stretched.

She'd improved vastly today. Her chest still ached, and

when she coughed, it was difficult to catch her breath, but she was almost certain her fever had abated.

Determined to prove to Cassius that she was well on her way to recovery, she carefully made her way toward the front of the cottage. The air had cooled considerably, and a shiver skittered across her shoulders.

Cassius had mentioned this forest was The South Pennines, and the temperature was always cooler here, particularly beneath the trees' leafy covering.

He must have heard her coming because he turned.

For an unguarded instant, he gazed at Beatrice with such longing and tenderness that she almost missed a step. In the next second, the shutters fell into place over his face with the swiftness of soldiers securing a bastion against marauders, and she might have imagined the desire written across his chiseled features.

Just as well.

How did two broken, beleaguered people traverse the rocky and uncertain path that was love? Wouldn't it be like the blind leading the blind?

After he'd assisted her back to her humble bed, he set about shuttering the windows. He'd already gone for water and there was naught else to do but wait until Layton and the others arrived.

He glanced at her before moving to the door. "All set?"

As much as she ever would be.

Beatrice gathered Teddy into her arms and pulled Nala close before giving a brave nod.

He searched her face, and for a heartbeat, she suspected he knew her embarrassing secret.

Thankfully, Cassius said nothing.

The hinges squeaked and groaned as he shoved the uneven door shut and slid a board into place to secure it.

Blackness as dark as the Earl of Hell's waistcoat enveloped her, and Beatrice breathed slowly in and out to prevent dread from overcoming her. Or at least she tried to. Instead of calm, even breaths, she panted as fear clawed its way up her spine.

Sweet Jesus.

It didn't matter that she wasn't alone. Curling her fingers into Nala's coat, she commanded her irregular gasps to subside.

As if sensing her inner turmoil, Teddy licked her chin.

Cassius must have heard Beatrice's panicked breathing, for before she could blink thrice in the inky darkness, he settled beside her. "Come here."

Then his arms encircled her, and Beatrice buried her face in his wide, comforting chest.

"I'm sorry," she murmured against the fine fabric of his shirt. "I know being afraid of the dark is silly at my age."

"*Hmm.*" He made that low humming sound in his chest that she'd come to adore.

"We all have fears, Beatrice." He stroked her back, up and down. "Have I told you about my grandmother, Libby the Dowager Duchess of Latham?"

A blatant change of subject to spare her further humiliation.

She adored Cassius for it.

"You've mentioned her." Beatrice tilted her head back, but it was impossible to see Cassius's face. Regardless, the warmth of his body and the steady *thump, thump* of his heart against her cheek reassured her.

"Lie back, and I'll tell you about her and the rest of my family." He chuckled, and she imagined the mirth lighting his dark blue eyes. "Grandmama is quite an eccentric old bird, but we all adore her and would do anything for her. She knows it too and isn't above exploiting our affection."

Soon, they lay side by side, face to face.

Nala tucked herself behind Beatrice's back, and Teddy rooted around near her feet before plopping down.

"Grandmama is part Roma, and she believes in all sorts of magical, mystical, unexplainable things..."

"She sounds like an exceptional woman." Beatrice fingered his waistcoat.

"That she is. You'll meet her when we reach Hefferwickshire."

Cassius continued to speak softly, telling Beatrice story after story about his grandmother. All the while, he held her in his arms and soothed her trembling with long, comforting strokes down her back.

Beatrice's fear gradually subsided, and her breathing settled into an even cadence as the night wore on. Surely it must be near midnight by now. Yawning, she snuggled closer, and it felt...right and natural...No, it felt perfect. She would cherish the memory of this night all her life.

Closing her eyes, she listened to Cassius's pleasant baritone until sleep carried her away.

A wet nose on her cheek woke her sometime later.

She lay cocooned beside Cassius, who snored softly near her ear.

"Teddy?" she murmured groggily.

"Holy hell!" Cassius bolted upright and dashed to the door, where he struggled with the board, acting as a barrier to intruders. "Something's gone wrong."

Light filtered in through a myriad of cracks in the walls.

Heart racing and mouth gone dry as parchment paper, Beatrice sat up, shoving her hair away from her face.

Oh, my God.

It's morning.

No one had come.

TWENTY

Still at the lodge

ABOUT HALF PAST SEVEN IN THE MORNING

If they had more supplies, Cassius wouldn't have considered what he was about to do. But they had no food left, and he couldn't risk using the ammunition for hunting. Besides, as much as he hated to admit it to Beatrice, he was a lousy hunter. As vulnerable as they were, remaining at the cottage was out of the question.

His conscience had berated him non-stop since awakening.

How could he have been so stupid as to have fallen asleep?

Unimaginable things might have occurred because of his lack of diligence.

It didn't matter that he hadn't slept more than a few minutes at a time for days.

Beatrice relied on him to keep her safe, and his failure to stay alert might have ended in disaster.

Without knowing what prevented Layton from returning, their only option was to set out for Hefferwickshire House and pray they didn't encounter anyone hostile.

He knew his eldest brother was a man of his word and fully capable of defending himself as well as covertly traveling rugged trails. He might not have been a spy as Lucius had been, but Layton had carried out several missions requiring stealth.

Something catastrophic must have kept him from returning last night, particularly since he knew full well exactly how dire Beatrice's situation was. Fear and apprehension wrestled for dominance, but Cassius couldn't allow Beatrice to see his concern. If they set out at once, they should make Hefferwickshire by this afternoon.

He prayed to God they would find Layton there, hale and hearty, with a plausible excuse for why he hadn't returned to the glen.

Still slightly wan from her illness, Beatrice eyed the horse with wide-eyed trepidation. She'd have to ride behind Cassius today, holding him around the waist. The rest of the journey would be rougher and more uneven, and he couldn't hold on to her and guide the horse at the same time.

If they needed to get away, she'd be safer behind him.

Double mounted, they would have to take it slow—far slower than he was comfortable with—which increased the risk of discovery. That and the fact that Cassius wasn't entirely positive he knew the route to take. He'd never been in this part of The South Pennines before.

Bloody hell, he swore silently.

Times like this, he wished he were more like his twin —any of his brothers, in truth. Even Althelia could out-shoot him. It was one thing to possess artistic talent, but that skill didn't lend itself to survival.

From a piece of a horse blanket, he'd contrived a sort of sling-type satchel for Beatrice to carry Teddy in. The little dog couldn't possibly travel on foot. The journey would test Nala's stamina and mettle, and she was far stronger and capable.

He wished he had something more to feed the dogs.

The gelding had munched on clumps of grass strewn around the glen yesterday and this morning. Thank God for that small favor. A weak, hungry mount could not take them to Hefferwickshire, and Beatrice wasn't recovered enough to walk. Nor would Cassius consider leaving her alone while he went for help.

They both either made it to their destination together, or both of them didn't.

It went against everything in him to make the horse bear him and Beatrice again, and he would have led the mount if he believed Beatrice could sit in the saddle on her own.

He didn't, and she couldn't.

Glancing around, he inhaled a deep, fortifying breath.

He didn't even know the horse's name.

There was still a chance—albeit small—they would encounter Layton and the others on the way, but Cassius's gut told him his optimism was misplaced. Fear for his brother rubbed his mind raw, but fretting about Layton right now would benefit no one.

The sooner Cassius and Beatrice reached the ducal estate, the sooner a search party could be mustered to look for Layton.

After this, Cassius planned on steering well clear of damsels in distress. If he'd wanted a life of adventure and peril, he'd have joined the military like Layton and Darius, been a spy like Lucius, run gambling clubs like Fletcher, or traveled the world and explored remote exotic locations as Leonidas did.

"I'm ready, Cassius."

As he saddled the horse, Beatrice had relieved herself.

She'd braided her hair and tied the end of the crimson and gold rope with a piece of cloth.

"I regret your having to travel in this fashion, Beatrice, when you are still recovering from your illness."

Would she relapse?

Would the strain of hard travel be too much for her to endure?

Cassius's mind recoiled from such thoughts.

He would ensure they reached Hefferwickshire House safely. He'd given his oath, but in his heart, he couldn't deny that it was much more than that.

Beatrice gave him a nascent smile, roving her gaze over his face, as if she wanted to graze her fingertips over his jaw, but didn't dare.

Part of him wished she would.

"Again, it is I who should be apologizing Cassius." The upward sweep of her lips turned stalwart, and a determined glint sparked in her eyes. "I shall manage perfectly well."

Cassius held his tongue, knowing full well that false bravado prompted her confident claim to hide her fear.

Water and a few berries comprised their meager rations to sustain them on the journey. Already hungry and tired, they needed to reach Hefferwickshire House today.

He slid the sling over Beatrice's slender neck and shoulder, then arranged it so that the pouch hung at her back. "Let's hope Teddy likes his travel accommodations."

"He'll be a good little lad." Her troubled gaze betrayed her doubt.

Cassius placed the confused dog in the sling.

At once, Teddy popped his head over the edge but did not climb out.

Cassius rubbed between his ears. "Good boy."

The pouch wiggled as Teddy wagged his tail.

"I'll boost you, Beatrice, and you shall sit behind the saddle. Hold on to the cantle—" at her bemused expression, he explained, "—the back, while I climb on."

Cassius had never mounted a horse with someone already sitting astride, but there was no way in hell Beatrice could manage on her own.

They would be lucky if they didn't both end up on their arses.

"I had a thought about that." She grimaced, looking like she'd swallowed a slug. "I have an idea. It's not exactly brilliant, but it may work."

As Brighton fell farther and farther behind them, her stutter continued to improve.

He supposed it was possible that Beatrice's uncle caused the nervousness that tongue-tied her, and that with him out of her life, her stutter would disappear too.

She gazed at Cassius expectantly, and he brought his thoughts back to the matter at hand.

He lifted an eyebrow, happy to hear anything that

could get them both atop the horse, uninjured. "I'm all ears."

"What if we moved the table outside? You could help me stand on it. Then, after you've mounted, I could straddle the horse."

It *was* brilliant.

For the first time since waking, he smiled. "Excellent idea."

It would mean leaving the table in the elements, but it was already in a sorry state, and it didn't look like the lodge's owner had used it in decades.

A couple of minutes later, they'd moved the less-than-sturdy table outdoors and braced it against the cottage.

"Here goes." Cassius lifted Beatrice onto the table, holding her steady as the ancient piece of furniture wobbled. She'd already rucked up her skirts, the brave darling.

She planted a hand against the shack's side and gave a valiant nod.

After climbing into the saddle, Cassius directed the horse to the table.

The animal shifted, adjusting its stance under his weight. Holding the reins in one palm, Cassius offered his other hand to Beatrice.

Teddy craned his neck, eager to see what went on.

Nala, on the other hand, appeared anxious and uncertain.

Gracing him with a grateful smile, Beatrice clasped his hand with unexpected strength and with surprising agility, clambered onto the gelding's back. She quickly wrapped her arms around Cassius's waist, and he doubted a debutante's tightened corset could squeeze his ribs any harder.

He didn't examine why his heart tripped over itself or why, despite the severity of their situation, his pulse quickened in joy and excitement. That either made him a libertine or a man on the verge of falling in love.

Neither made him happy.

Nala cocked her head, one ear lifted.

They must be quite a sight.

Looking over his shoulder, Cassius gave Beatrice an encouraging smile. "No talking. Voices carry in the woods."

She nodded and then snapped her fingers.

Nala immediately came to her side.

With a soft click of his tongue, Cassius murmured, "Walk on."

God only knew what the next few hours would bring.

TWENTY-ONE

The primary route from
Carlisle to Cumberland

SIX HOURS LATER

The horse's rocking plod came to a stop, rousing Beatrice from a fitful doze. Too afraid to sleep, lest she tumble from the gelding, she hovered on the brink of slumber with her cheek pressed against Cassius's broad back the past few hours as the horse picked its way over the uneven terrain.

Despite the troubling circumstances, she had to admit she rather enjoyed snuggling up to Cassius's back. As it was unlikely she'd ever embrace such a fine specimen of masculinity again, she kicked aside any guilt for indulging.

How different things might have been if he hadn't buried his heart in his work, and she hadn't determined long ago to remain a spinster.

Ah, well...

Blinking sleepily, Beatrice lifted her head and peered around.

A road. A proper road.

And a well-traveled one at that.

Thank God, they'd made it to the principal route to Cumberland. That meant Cassius's familial home lay less than twenty miles away. By nightfall, she would be clean, sated from a good meal, and resting in a comfortable bed, and her fears of Uncle Cedric's men overtaking them gradually fading away.

If the rest of the trip was as uneventful as the past few hours.

Now that they must travel on a road, there was a greater risk of discovery if Uncle Cedric persisted in trying to apprehend her.

Intuition told her he would not give up, but she was no closer to understanding why her uncle was so bent on seeing her married than she had been when this fiasco started in Brighton.

Teddy whined and fidgeted in the sling behind her.

Beatrice coughed into her shoulder, but her chest didn't hurt anymore.

No doubt, the dog, like her, could use a few minutes

of privacy. If the Good Lord showed her any favor, she would never again for as long as she drew breath, have to hide behind a bush to see to her personal needs.

Instead of riding straight onto the road, ever vigilant, Cassius lingered in the shadow of the trees. With his forefinger raised in warning to keep silent, he scanned the area.

Sitting up tall on the horse, Beatrice craned her neck to see past his shoulders and peered up and down the dusty track.

Nothing disturbed the summer afternoon's calmness.

"Is it safe?" she murmured in Cassius's ear, still fearful of being overheard.

Her voice came out a throaty scratch, as much from being silent for hours as recovering from her cold.

He gave a slow nod. "I think so."

How she longed to have the right to soothe the lines of fatigue from his dear face.

"Before we continue, do you need a few minutes alone?" he asked.

A discreet way of inquiring if Beatrice needed to relieve herself.

She did.

Quite desperately, in truth.

No doubt, he did too, though how she would get back onto the horse might prove challenging.

"Yes, please." Beatrice ought to be mortified about

discussing something so personal, but pride had a way of evaporating when critical matters shoved themselves to the forefront. At that precise moment, her very full bladder didn't give two figs about her delicate sensibilities.

An overly full bladder wasn't her only discomfort. Her stomach seemed intent on gnawing through her spinal column. For all the suffering she'd endured at Uncle Cedric's hand, she'd been well-fed.

Except for the times he'd punished her by sending her to bed without supper. Sometimes, a kind servant sneaked her a dinner roll or an apple to hold her over until morning. If her uncle had caught them, the servant would have faced immediate dismissal, which explained why, most of the time, no one dared try to help her.

In short order, Cassius dismounted, lifted her down, and set Teddy on the ground.

Almost afraid to move, lest her bottom scream in protest or her legs buckle beneath her, as they had the other night, Beatrice took a couple of tentative steps. To be sure, she was sore, and her inner thighs chafed, but the discomfort was bearable this time.

Cassius led the gelding back into the trees for privacy, and she hurried behind a fallen log. After inspecting the area to ensure no one and nothing observed her, Beatrice attended to her needs.

Once finished, she tried to brush the grime from her

stained clothing. What an unkempt state to be in to meet the Duke and Duchess of Latham. She hoped Cassius's parents were as understanding and welcoming as he'd assured Beatrice they were.

Still, arriving at a ducal estate wearing soiled and tattered garments, smelling of horse and sweat, and in dire need of a bath, wasn't exactly the introduction to Cassius's parents Beatrice had anticipated.

They might mistake her for a tatterdemalion—or worse—rather than an heiress.

What would they think of her, involving their son in her troubles?

Beatrice's welcome might not be as cordial as Cassius assured her it would be.

Still, she had no choice but to continue onward.

Coming out from behind the fallen larch tree, she signaled Nala and Teddy to her side. All she needed was for one dog to chase a squirrel or rabbit and delay the journey.

Several feet away, Cassius stared at the road, visible through the forest.

Was he concerned?

Should she be too?

As if he'd been listening for her, Cassius glanced in Beatrice's direction. His expression unreadable, he held his hand up, clearly telling her to be still.

She froze in place, fear nearly strangling her, then

snapped her fingers twice; the signal for her dogs to remain immobile.

Uncle Cedric had poked fun at her for spending so much time training Nala and Teddy, but her efforts had not been for nothing. This moment was proof.

A cart, pulled by a pair of mismatched but sturdy horses, lumbered down the track toward them. Cheerful, off-key whistling carried into the serene woods where the birds had stopped singing.

In short order, a beefy man wearing humble farmer's clothing, along with a lad of perhaps fourteen dozing beside him, trundled past. The wagon bed contained several metal milk cans that clinked and clanked against each other on the bumpy road.

Once the cart disappeared from sight, Cassius brought the gelding near the tree next to which Beatrice stood rooted.

"A local dairy farmer taking his milk to market in Kirby Lonsdale," he explained. "My ancestral home is only about five miles from here."

In the process of lifting Teddy into her arms, Beatrice jerked her head up. "*Only five?*"

That was so much better than the twenty, she'd guessed.

Relief tunneled through her veins.

This leg of her journey to freedom was nearly over.

"Aye. Mayhap a little less. We'll cut through the

woods and a couple of meadows." Scratching his temple, Cassius grinned as he maneuvered the horse into place for her to climb on. "I recognized where I was several miles back and took a diagonal route through the woodlands. My father's land borders this road for the next several miles."

Miles?

Just how big was the ducal estate?

"All we have to do is cross the road a few feet farther along, and we are on private property. Not even your uncle's men would be stupid enough to try to apprehend us on the Duke of Latham's land."

Beatrice wasn't so certain because she didn't know what motivated her uncle to begin with.

"Beatrice, would you like to sit in the saddle for a while?"

Cassius's question took her off guard.

The crooked smile he bestowed upon her gave him an almost bashful, boyish appearance. "It's only slightly more comfortable than riding behind me."

Or on his lap?

A little thrill she certainly ought not to have felt, let alone enjoyed, zipped along her veins at the thought.

Again, he considered her needs above his own. However, Beatrice's primary concern was getting to Hefferwickshire House as quickly as possible and without acting like a moon-eyed ninny along the way.

She'd not risk her friendship with him by having him discover her feelings had grown into something considerably warmer than platonic over the past few days.

Aiming for a practical mien, she adjusted Teddy in her arms and asked, "Which is the fastest way for us to travel?"

The small dog panted, his little pink tongue hanging from his mouth as the temperature rose, even in the trees' shade. In truth, she considered removing her cloak and using it as additional padding between her and the horse.

Except, with her gown hitched up, that meant exposing her bare calves and part of her thighs. She wasn't quite daring enough for that.

Rubbing Teddy's head, Cassius considered her question.

"I'm not an expert on these things." He brushed a hand over his bristly jaw.

That was another thing she appreciated about him. He didn't try to be a know-it-all or puff up with self-importance by pretending knowledge or skills he didn't have.

"In truth, I've only ever ridden double with you," he said.

Beatrice couldn't prevent the slight slackening of her mouth in surprise.

She'd assumed with as many siblings as Cassius had, and having come from a family where riding was as natural as walking, he'd have experienced riding double many times. It just proved how ignorant she was of not only horseback riding but of his life and family.

"But I'd guess it would be swifter with you behind me again since I'm experienced with holding the reins and you are not." He gathered Teddy into his arms. "Which means, little chap, it's back into the sling for you."

Once he'd tucked Teddy into his pouch, Cassius helped balance Beatrice as she swung a very sore leg over the horse's broad back.

She barely suppressed a groan. But she vowed not to complain. Regardless, a very long soak in a steaming bath was definitely in order.

Beatrice tried not to notice when Cassius accidentally brushed his arm across her breasts as he slid into the saddle. A jolt of sensation shot to her stomach at the contact, proving what she accepted these past couple of days.

She was attracted to him.

More than attracted, truthfully.

But what woman would not be?

Had it been any other man, she might've suspected him of touching her breasts deliberately, but Cassius had only ever been the perfect gentleman toward her.

Which, in point of fact, had become the teensiest bit frustrating.

Twice now, she thought he might kiss her. But each

time, he refrained and retreated behind his wall of politeness and impeccable manners.

One kiss wouldn't turn the world on its axis, wouldn't stop the tides from changing or the moon from rising. But one kiss *would* be a treasure she could hide away in her heart, and when loneliness and regret reared their gnarly little heads as they were bound to do, she would have Cassius's kiss to retrieve from its fusty hiding place and savor what never could have been.

She stared at his raven hair teasing the collar of his jacket.

I'll have that kiss before we part ways, Cassius Westbrook.

You just wait and see.

Beatrice's tummy fluttered at her naughty vow, but she meant it.

Someway, somehow, she would share a kiss with this man.

Once they left the woods' protective cover, Cassius steered the tired horse to the right.

The poor creature moved slower now, having borne the brunt of carrying two people and a dog for many hours. The gelding deserved extra grain, a long rub down, and a thorough brushing.

For the next half hour, they rode in silence, only the calls, chirps, and tweets of birds and squirrels interrupting the serenity of their surroundings. Several times, Beatrice couldn't prevent a swift glance behind them to assure herself they weren't about to be overtaken by ruffians.

Tension eased from her shoulders when Cassius turned the horse off the main track into another wooded area interspersed with small stands of birch and oak. They disturbed a red stag lying in the two-foot-high grass, and the noble creature bolted for the forest's safety.

Trying to ignore her sore inner thighs, Beatrice inhaled a cleansing breath, almost heady with relief.

They were finally safe—well, as safe as they would be until they reached the manor house.

"Cassius, are you certain your parents shan't be put out when we show up on their doorstep unannounced?" It wasn't likely the duke and duchess would object to their son's arrival.

But hers?

That might prove to be a wholly different scenario.

"I would hate to be an imposition." Beatrice flexed her fingers against his ribs, and he shifted.

His shoulders shook, and it took her a moment to realize he was laughing.

Because he was ticklish or because of her question?

"What, pray tell, is so blasted funny Cassius Westbrook?" She dug her fingers into his ribs again.

"I'm sorry." He glanced over his shoulder, those beautiful dark blue eyes sparkling with humor.

He didn't look the least bit sorry.

"My parents live for occasions like this. I assure you, they love nothing better than to rescue someone. It makes them feel needed."

Beatrice mulled that over for several *clip-clops* of the horse's hooves.

How very different were the duke and duchess from her uncle, who detested helping anyone.

"Tell me more about them, please." She rested her chin on his back.

Such familiarity was beyond the pale, but after all they had endured over the past few days, propriety had flown out the window. Every detail she learned about him was another trinket she could store in the treasure chest of her heart.

"It will help me feel less intimidated when I finally meet them." That much was true.

"Father and Mother were both married before. My oldest brothers, Layton and Fletcher, were from Mother's first marriage. Father adopted them when they were quite young." Affection threaded his voice before he chuckled. "You shouldn't be surprised to learn my grandmama had a hand in their union."

"Your part Roma grandmother, the dowager duchess?"

"Aye." He half turned in the saddle. "She's a meddling old dear, so watch yourself. She's not above shenanigans to get her way either."

"I shall take your advice to heart." Beatrice couldn't prevent her answering grin.

Nala trotted ahead, seemingly no worse the wear from her long trek.

Cassius's family sounded lovely.

How wonderful it must've been to grow up surrounded by siblings and with loving parents.

Another half hour passed as he chatted about his sister, six brothers, the duke and duchess, and his grandmother.

"She tricked us all into coming home for Christmas that year." He shook his head. "We were all convinced something ghastly had occurred or that she was dying."

They exited the woodland into a lush meadow and across the way, stood a majestic manor, more castle than house.

Beatrice couldn't contain her gasp or the involuntary tightening of her arms around his middle.

"Oh, Cassius. Your family home is magnificent."

"I never tire of coming home." Pride deepened his voice. "No matter what might happen while I am away, this place lifts my spirits every time."

A noise farther along the meadow drew her attention, and she slid a casual glance in that direction.

A pair of rough-looking men thundered from the tree line. Even at this distance, she could see the menace contorting their unshaven faces.

No. Not now.

Not when we are so close.

"Cassius? There are two men—"

His curse cut off her warning.

"Hold tight, Beatrice. We must make a break for the house."

TWENTY-TWO

Hefferwickshire House's lands

A COUPLE OF TERRIFYING HEARTBEATS LATER

Cassius didn't need to look twice to know the men were up to no good. Their unmitigated gall in trespassing on ducal lands suggested the Earl of Highbury had offered a substantial reward for Beatrice's return.

Digging his heels into the horse's sides, he whistled—a high-pitched series of notes. He repeated the whistle several times as they barreled toward the house.

And he prayed someone would hear the signal and sound the alarm.

All the Westbrooks had learned the whistle when they

were children. Father had insisted upon it, and the staff knew it meant danger. Or a potential abduction. That someone was hurt or needed help. A fire... Any manner of peril.

Beatrice clung to him, her breath coming in frantic little pants.

"Nala," she cried. "Come."

Nala sprinted beside the horse.

Cassius held no false hope that this weary beast could outrun the miscreants' horses.

He whistled the alarm again.

And again.

A shout went up from the stables.

Then another. And another.

An answering whistle carried from the estate.

Thank God.

"Help is coming, Beatrice."

He shot a frantic glance over his shoulder.

The thugs closed in on them.

One raised a pistol.

Holy Hell.

Mayhap the earl didn't want her back alive, after all.

The villain lowered the barrel, aiming at the lagging horse.

"The blackguard means to take the horse down, Beatrice. Hang on."

Cassius would die before he let those men get their hands on her.

He veered the horse to the right, and then to the left.

A gunshot rang out.

A small shriek escaped Beatrice as she dug her nails into his stomach. She squeezed him so tightly that he doubted an ant could crawl between them.

Teddy yipped in terror.

"Oh, God. Help us," she cried in a strangled voice.

Nala barked and bared her teeth.

The horse's lathered sides heaved.

The poor beast couldn't continue much longer.

Another shot reverberated through the air.

Cassius braced himself for the horse to stumble, but it continued onward, stretching its legs out in a manner that would credit any Ascot champion.

By God, he would buy this animal, and the gelding would live the rest of his days in luxury and comfort at Hefferwickshire.

The creature had proven himself ten times over.

The thunder of hooves echoed as riders approached from the house, hell-bent-for-nothing.

His Father and brothers, Fletcher and Adolphus, were among the riders along with several stable hands. They must've been about to go for a ride or just returned from one, given the many saddled horses. Behind them, at least a half dozen more men charged across the field on foot.

"Cassius," Beatrice gasped into his ear. "The m-men... They've turned around and are f-fleeing in the other d-direction."

A swift glance over his shoulder verified the cowards had indeed tucked their tails and were making their escape.

Sweat ran in rivulets down his face and soaked his shirt.

His heart beat an irregular staccato behind his ribs.

That had been too bloody close.

If he and Beatrice hadn't been near the house...

The consequences were too horrific to consider.

His father, brothers, and three men raced to meet him while another five continued on in pursuit of the hench-men. There was little chance they'd catch them, and Highbury's hirelings would escape to report back to the earl.

"Are you both unharmed?" Father skimmed his worried gaze over him before darting a concerned glance toward Beatrice. "Miss Fairfax, I presume?"

Naturally, his father would make the connection as Cassius had asked for his help regarding her inheritance.

"We're fine now, thanks to you, Father. And yes, this is Beatrice Fairfax." He squeezed her fingers, still digging into his ribs. "I'll perform proper introductions later."

"Your Grace." Fear and perhaps awe at meeting the Duke of Latham rendered Beatrice's voice a faint, reedy sound. She rested heavily against Cassius. "I apologize for this debacle."

As if it were in any way her fault.

She'd rotated the sling forward and lifted Teddy from his enclosure. "My dog."

At once, Maddock hurried forward and accepted the wriggling bundle of ebony fur. "Hello, little laddie. Aren't ye a handsome wee fellow?"

"The horse is hit." Adolphus made that shocked observation.

What?

Pivoting in the saddle, Cassius bent to see where his brother pointed.

Sure enough, scarlet covered the poor beast's side.

"Good God!" Fletcher leaped from his horse and hurtled toward Cassius and Beatrice. "It's not the horse. It's Miss Fairfax who's been shot."

No. No. No.

Something unnamed shattered inside Cassius.

He met Beatrice's pain-filled hazel eyes.

"I believe I've taken a ball to the thigh," she whispered, as though surprised by the revelation.

Her eyelids fluttered as she slipped sideways from the horse.

Fletcher caught her, then lowered her to the ground.

As he swiftly dismounted, Father signaled to one of the nearby men. "Go for Doctor Hartney at once. And send a wagon back for Miss Fairfax. Also, alert the house. Tell the duchess to prepare a chamber."

Bent low over the horse's neck, Farrel, one of Hefferwickshire's coachmen, raced for the mansion.

With his heart in his throat and buzzing in his ears, Cassius slid off the horse and tossed the reins to Tobie, another stable hand. "See to it that he has the very best care. He saved our lives."

"Yes, my lord." Tobie bobbed his head and ran a hand down the horse's lathered neck.

Cassius dropped to his knees beside Beatrice.

"Beatrice. My Beatrice. Oh, God."

Was that raw, savage cry from him?

Using his body to shield her from curious stares, he yanked her skirts up. Crimson covered her ivory left thigh and a miniature river flowed from a nasty gash.

That was why she'd cried out, and yet she'd managed to stay on the horse.

His heart swelled with pride and love for her.

Yes, love.

Cassius loved Beatrice.

Admiration thrummed through him, quickly followed by searing fear.

She must be all right. She must.

He hadn't told her how he felt.

How could he when he'd just realized the truth himself?

Fletcher kneeled beside him and, having already removed his neckcloth, tied it around her leg to form a tourniquet. He had practiced medicine before walking away from the profession over a decade before. "Father, your cravat, please. We need to stop the bleeding. She's already lost too much blood."

At once, the duke handed over his perfectly starched neckcloth.

Her face translucent, Beatrice remained unresponsive.

"You have to save her, Fletcher." The broken, tormented whisper ripped from Cassius's throat. "I...I love her."

TWENTY-THREE

A luxurious bedchamber
Hefferwickshire House

MID-MORNING THE NEXT DAY

Lying on surely what must be a cloud and not a mattress, with lavender and lilac scented sheets pulled up to her neck, Beatrice slowly and reluctantly left Morpheus's arms. A half-smile of contentment bending her mouth, she stirred and stretched.

Searing pain ripped through her left thigh, and a little yelp escaped her.

Sweet Jesus on Sunday.

Her eyelids flew open, and she stared at the unfamiliar pleats of a sage-green canopy.

Where was she?

Why did her leg hurt so confounded awful, and why was she so weak?

Her memory came flooding back in a rush.

Men chasing Cassius and me.

A gunshot.

Molten agony impaling my leg.

Cassius's family arriving and scaring the thugs away.

Blood. So much blood.

Cassius whispering my name.

And then...nothing.

Teddy stirred and crawled from the foot of the bed to rest his ebony head on her shoulder. He sighed, his good brown eye round with worry.

"Hello, my little friend." Beatrice stroked his back. "Where's your sister?"

A large snout nuzzled her elbow, and if Beatrice hadn't been in so much pain, she might've laughed. She scratched under Nala's chin.

"I love you too, Nala."

"Ah, you are awake. I thought I heard you." A tall, stunning auburn-haired woman fairly glided into the bedchamber. Everything about her, from her coral and emerald gown to the small emerald earrings dangling from her earlobes, screeched nobility. "I'm Margaret Westbrook, the Duchess of Latham. Are you thirsty, my dear?"

"Yes, Your Grace." Beatrice's voice came out a rough croak, but thankfully, she did not stutter despite her nerves. She cleared her throat and gratefully accepted the water the duchess poured for her.

After drinking every drop, she passed the glass back.

To her surprise, the duchess refilled it and extended it once more. "Fletcher says it's important to drink lots of water after blood loss."

"Fletcher?" Beatrice dutifully lifted the glass to her lips and drained the contents once more.

He was the one who had studied medicine, wasn't he?

"Yes. He cleaned your wound and stitched the gash. Though the laceration is quite deep, the lead ball grazed the soft tissue, which, my son tells me, is the best type of bullet injury to have." The duchess carefully lowered herself onto the embroidered sage and ivory counterpane. "Even so, you'll be confined to bed for a couple of weeks. Doctor Hartney shall be along shortly to check on you."

Why not Fletcher?

Flicking a long, elegant finger toward a small brown bottle on the nightstand, Her Grace said, "Fletcher left a bottle of laudanum for pain. Do you need a dose?"

Beatrice considered her discomfort for a moment.

As long as she lay still, the pain was bearable.

Afraid to jar her leg, she gave the teensiest shake of her head. "Not right now, thank you. Perhaps later if the pain worsens."

Her grace laid a perfumed hand against Beatrice's fore-head. She smelled as lovely as she appeared. Cassius hadn't exaggerated either. His mother was the epitome of kindness.

"Excellent. No fever." The Duchess of Latham smiled broadly, revealing perfect white teeth. "I am so relieved. Cassius fretted something awful because he said you had been quite ill, and fever after a bullet injury is worrisome."

"Thanks to Cassius and Layton's care, I was already on the mend."

Before being shot, that is.

Emotion flickered across the duchess's face, but she swiftly schooled her features into a pleasant mien. For a woman just past her sixth decade, she had remarkably few lines. Just a few fine creases around the outer edges of her eyes and bracketing her mouth when she smiled. Still slen-der, despite having birthed eight children, she possessed a figure many younger women would envy.

Beatrice smoothed her hands across the sheet, neatly folded over the lush counterpane, noticing for the first time the lace-edged sleeves of the light blue silk nightgown she wore.

The duchess's or perhaps Cassius's sister's garment?

No, Althelia had married and lived with her husband now.

This nightgown must belong to her grace.

Beatrice slid a curious glance around the room, taking in the décor.

The chamber they'd given her was breathtakingly beautiful.

Elegant wallpaper adorned with a lovely design of flowers, leaves, and vines upon an ivory background covered three walls. The matching rosewood four-poster bed, armoire, dressing table, writing desk, and floral upholstered chairs bespoke understated wealth and luxury. Several plants, including ferns and a rubber plant placed around the room, gave the chamber an almost tropical atmosphere.

A petite, raven-haired woman popped her head into the room. Her blue eyes fairly sparked with energy as she came to stand at the foot of the bed.

"So you decided to rejoin the living," she said in a lovely Irish burr. "I'm Siobhan Westbrook, Fletcher's wife."

This was the woman who had pretended to be a boy at Fletcher Westbrook's social club so she could earn a living to care for her younger brother and sister.

Cassius had told Beatrice all about his siblings and their spouses.

What a fascinating family.

"Our patient is awake at last, *non*?" Another beauty entered the chamber. From her French accent, Beatrice assumed she was Aurelie Westbrook, the Marchioness of

Edenhaven and future Duchess of Latham. She gingerly perched on the other side of the bed. "*Zut*, you gave us quite a scare, Miss Fairfax."

"I'm so sorry to be such an inconvenience." Arriving in a frazzled, dirty state was one thing. Being hauled in bleeding and unconscious was another entirely.

"None of that flimflam." The duchess waved an elegant hand. "I know I speak for all of us when I say how very glad we are that the men chased those scoundrels off."

The three women gazed at Beatrice, expectation in their eyes, but they were too polite to ask the obvious question.

"My uncle, the Earl of Highbury, sent those men." Beatrice glanced toward the door.

Where was Cassius?

Had he checked on her at all?

In her fevered state at the cabin, she'd overheard him tell Layton that as soon as they arrived at Hefferwickshire House, he meant to wash his hands of her.

Had he already done so?

A lump formed in her throat, and she swallowed hard to dislodge it.

Thump-thump. Thump-thump.

Eyes twinkling, the duchess patted Beatrice's hand.

"Ah, I hear my mother-in-law, Elizabeth. Everyone calls her Libby," she told Beatrice with a confidential smile before raising her voice and calling, "We're in Beatrice's chamber, Mother Westbrook."

Tinkling accompanied the uneven gait as the thumping grew louder.

A petite, plump woman wearing spectacles appeared in the doorway, leaning heavily on a cane.

Beatrice counted no fewer than six pendants hanging from her neck, nine bracelets on her wrists, and five feathers, each a different color, in her silver hair. Long, ornate earrings, more befitting a gypsy dancer, dangled from her earlobes.

The dowager duchess toddled a few steps farther into the chamber before pointing her ivory-handled cane at Beatrice. "You're the niece of that sniveling whelp, Highbury?"

Disdain for Uncle Cedric radiated from her fragile form.

How did she know Uncle Cedric well enough to know what a rotter he was?

"I am, ma'am."

"*Hmph.* I knew your grandmother well." She gave a sage nod, causing the feathers in her hair to bob in unison. "Your mother too. Sweet gel, though a bit flighty."

Well, that answered that question.

She peered at Beatrice for several long seconds. "I must say, you are not at all what I expected."

"I'm sorry to disappoint, Your Grace." How else could Beatrice respond?

The dowager broke into raspy laughter which sounded like old paper crinkling, and the sisters-in-laws exchanged amused, tolerant glances.

"Don't be a dunderhead, girl. That was meant as a compliment." Still chuckling, the elderly dame shuffled closer. "I feared Highbury had ruined you, but I see you have your grandmother's spunk. Good thing. Had you been sweet and compliant like your mother, Highbury would've squashed you."

Thank you, didn't seem an appropriate reply, so Beatrice fashioned a polite smile.

"I found Highbury's irrational jealousy toward your mother worrisome, even when they were children." The dowager curled her lip when she mentioned Uncle Cedric. "Your grandmother tried to protect your mother, but he was a sly lad. Grew into an even craftier adult."

So Uncle Cedric had been jealous of Mama.

"When Euphemia didn't disinherit Seraphina, but instead, provided for her and you, the earl nearly had an apoplexy." The dowager was a veritable fountain of information. "Highbury thought for certain the scandal surrounding your birth would ensure he inherited all his mother's money too, greedy sod."

Her unexpected revelation explained why Uncle

Cedric couldn't bear any mention of Mama. His jealousy had driven him to madness, it seemed.

"Mother Westbrook," the Duchess of Latham gently chastised. "Are you certain now is the right time for this?"

"The girl deserves to know the truth. Besides, she's no wilting wallflower, are you, dear?"

Beatrice shook her head, liking the unconventional woman immensely.

"*Hmph*. I thought not. You have pluck and gumption. *I* can tell." The dowager placed both hands atop her cane handle before continuing her sordid tale. "When Euphemia found out Highbury had bribed that Italian miscreant to ruin your mother..."

Beatrice sat up straighter, wincing as her leg protested the sudden movement.

He did what?

Uncle Cedric was behind Mama's ruination?

The cad. Blackguard, Scoundrel. Villain.

Fury tunneled through Beatrice.

The man was truly irredeemable—rotten to the core. What was more, he'd turned his hatred of Mama onto Beatrice. If anyone deserved to burn in hell, it was Cedric Fairfax, Seventh Earl of Highbury. If she never saw the wretch again, it would be too soon.

Firming her mouth into a thin ribbon, the elderly dame shook her silvery head again, once more sending her feathers into fisticuffs with each other. "I tell you,

Euphemia was a shrewd and intelligent woman. She made certain Highbury would never see a farthing of her money."

The dowager duchess chuckled again, but a fit of coughing interrupted her laughter.

"Perhaps a cup of tea with honey is in order, Grandmama, *non*?" Aurelie suggested.

Beatrice angled another surreptitious glance toward the door.

Not furtive enough, however.

"Cassius and the others aren't here, my dear."

TWENTY-FOUR

*A COUPLE OF HUMILIATING HEARTBEATS
LATER*

The duchess's sympathetic smile caused dual streaks of heat to skate up Beatrice's cheeks.

Was she so obvious?

Pining for a man who didn't want her?

"Oh, I merely wanted to th-thank Mr. Westbrook for caring for m-my injury," she fibbed. "And the others t-too, of course."

Blast her stutter.

It gave her away as plainly as if she'd declared, "*Yes, I want to see Cassius. I adore him.*"

A compassionate smile framing her mouth, Siobhan

came around the bed and cautiously sat on the edge opposite the duchess.

"I'm afraid that will have to wait," her grace said, kindly. "The men have all gone to search for my eldest son, Layton."

Beatrice snapped her head up. "What has happened? Cassius vowed something awful must have occurred to keep Captain Westbrook from returning with help for us."

The women exchanged cautious glances.

"Cassius told us how Layton came to your aid." A tightness entered the duchess's features.

"Y-yes." Guilt speared Beatrice, and she could barely form a coherent sentence. "Cassius and I encountered h-him at an inn on a back road from B-Brighton."

Curses. Stop stuttering.

Concentrating on each word, Beatrice spoke slowly but clearly. "He joined us on our journey to Hefferwickshire House, but I became too ill to travel. After spending the night in a hunting lodge, Cassius and Captain Westbrook decided Captain Westbrook should go for help."

The Duchess, her daughters-in-law, and the dowager traded another round of knowing glances.

Because staying with two men unchaperoned, utterly compromised Beatrice?

Or because they blamed her for Captain Westbrook's disappearance?

She plucked at the coverlet.

"He never returned," Beatrice said in a small voice. "Cassius was frantic with worry."

"Layton was abducted." The epitome of regal self-control, the duchess swallowed. She couldn't hide the fear shining in her green eyes, though. "We received a ransom note."

Sitting up, Beatrice gasped as much from shock as from the sudden movement.

"That's horrible." They all must be terrified for him. "I'm so sorry."

Surely her uncle's hoodlums weren't involved in the abduction.

It must be a coincidence, though it was unusual to abscond with a noble's adult child. Most aristocratic kidnappings involved children. She couldn't imagine Layton was giving his abductors an easy time of it, either, which might prove more dangerous for him.

Her empty stomach took that inopportune moment to growl with the ferocity of a starving African lion, and mortification swept over her as she laid a hand over her rebellious belly.

"Get the girl something to eat." The dowager duchess banged her cane on the undeserving floor. "She sounds hollow to her spine. How can she heal if she's starving?"

The marchioness stood, and Siobhan rose as well.

"I'll go to the kitchen and prepare a tray," the future duchess said.

"And I'll ask for warm water so that you may wash. Fletcher said you cannot get the wound wet, but you may sponge off the rest of your body." Siobhan crinkled her nose as she recited her husband's orders. "I shall help you wash your hair in a couple of days if you'd like, provided you're feeling up to it."

"I've had Mrs. Tastespotting prepare soup, custard, and fresh bread." The duchess patted Beatrice's shoulder. "I'm glad you are here, Miss Fairfax."

"Please, call me Beatrice." She fashioned a brave, if somewhat wobbly smile, and glanced at each woman. "I appreciate everything you've done for me, but I'm accustomed to seeing to my own needs. I'm certain you have other, more important matters to attend to."

The dowager duchess chuckled. "We were given explicit orders by *your* Cassius to take excellent care of you."

Another blush stole up Beatrice's face.

She must look like a cooked lobster.

"Oh, he's not *my* Cassius." Where did the old dear get that peculiar notion?

Beatrice twisted the lace adorning the top sheet. "He's been very kind and helpful, and if not for him, I don't know what would have happened to me. But I assure you, we're merely friends. Nothing more."

The skeptical glances between the four women showed they didn't believe a word of Beatrice's declaration.

"If you say so dear." The merry glint in the dowager's cloudy blue eyes belied her acquiescence. "I shall come back this afternoon and we can have a pleasant chat about your grandmother and mother." She raised her nose an inch. "I doubt Cedric had anything kind to say about Seraphina."

She truly knew Uncle Cedric's character.

The Westbrook women made their way toward the doorway.

Beatrice vacillated between her desire to accept the kindness of these lovely people and convalesce in such beautiful surroundings and worrying about being a burden to the Westbrook family.

Cassius wasn't even here to act as a buffer. The fear that he and his father and brothers would return without Captain Westbrook weighed heavily upon her mind. Her stomach tightened into a knot at the prospect.

What if she had inadvertently caused his brother's demise?

She would never forgive herself if Captain Westbrook died, and she doubted his family would forgive her, either.

Wouldn't it be better to leave then?

Before they asked her to?

Yes. Yes, it would.

Beatrice bit her lip in indecision then blurted, "Your Grace?"

"Yes?" The duchess half-turned, one regal auburn eyebrow raised.

"I don't wish to be an imposition. If I might have paper and ink, I can write to the solicitor in London about my inheritance." Beatrice offered what she hoped was a confident smile, even though with every word, her heart cracked a little more. "I'm sure he can provide other arrangements for me."

A lump formed in her throat, and she swallowed twice.

She felt like a tremendous inconvenience, though the thought of leaving without saying goodbye to Cassius and thanking him for everything he'd done for her, brought stinging tears rushing to her eyes. What was more, she would never claim that glorious kiss she'd promised herself.

Lowering her gaze so the women wouldn't jump to an accurate conclusion about why she was weepy, she wrestled her emotions into submission.

"Nonsense. I shan't hear of you leaving." Though the duchess's tone was gentle, an underlying steeliness weighted her denial. "Besides, it will be at least a fortnight before you are up and walking without assistance."

A fortnight?

Well, that would give Beatrice plenty of time to contemplate her future and make appropriate plans.

Surely Cassius would have returned by then.

"I think a letter to your solicitor can wait a few days too." The Duchess of Latham gave Beatrice a motherly smile.

Beatrice liked her.

She wasn't the least pretentious or snooty.

"You should concentrate on recovering, my dear." Again, it wasn't so much as a suggestion as a dictate from her grace. "Everything else can wait."

Not when you had a mad-as-the-devil uncle.

If all the Westbrook men were away, just who, precisely, guarded the house?

Surely, Cassius elucidated how persistent and determined Uncle Cedric was.

Wouldn't this be a perfect opportunity for her uncle's men to return and potentially cause more harm? Perhaps even snatch her?

"Your Grace? Did Cassius explain about my uncle?" Beatrice plucked at the sheets with her fingertips. "I don't want to put anyone at Hefferwickshire House in danger."

Her very presence did precisely that.

The dowager poked her head around her daughter-in-law. "If that blackguard tries anything nefarious, we are prepared. Never fear. Highbury's always been a coward though. That's why he has others do his dirty work."

"We have things well in hand, Beatrice." The Duchess of Latham slipped her mother-in-law's hand into the crook of her elbow. "My husband saw to our security before he left. I assure you, we are well protected."

Beatrice ought to be relieved, but she couldn't relax until she had her inheritance in hand.

"I'll see what is keeping your luncheon." Leaving the bedchamber door open, the duchess escorted her mother down the corridor.

After they'd gone, Beatrice relaxed against the fluffy pillows and let her mind wander to yesterday, after being shot. In the moments before oblivion had completely claimed her, she swore she'd heard Cassius say he loved her.

If he cared for her, why had he left without saying goodbye or, at the very least, leaving a note?

Because the truth was, it changed nothing.

He meant to foist her off on his parents, and what better way to do it than to leave straightaway, even if the circumstances were dire?

Her heart shattering at the undeniable truth, Beatrice closed her eyes as a lone tear leaked from the corner of one eye and trailed down her cheek. She would insist on writing to Hargreaves & Drummond and request a meeting at Hefferwickshire House with all haste.

"If I don't hear from Cassius, then as soon as I can walk, I shall leave."

Teddy whined and laid his head on his paws while Nala planted her large muzzle on the bed and gazed at Beatrice with woeful eyes.

"Not a bit of it. You shan't make me feel guilty. I'm not the one who hied away faster than a beggar with a stolen loaf of bread." She shook her head. "He didn't even leave a note."

Which could only mean one thing.

He didn't care.

She must have imagined his declaration of love.

TWENTY-FIVE

Hefferwickshire House

NINETEEN DAYS LATER ~ JUST AFTER NOON

Bone-weary and his heart heavy, Cassius plodded up Hefferwickshire House's front steps. Exhausted, Father had come home last week. Adolphus, Lucius, and their cousin Torrian Westbrook, also a private investigator, continued to search for Layton.

These past weeks hadn't been in vain. They had located the abductors, but Layton had already escaped captivity and then disappeared without a trace.

Cassius hadn't given up hope and prayed daily that Layton would be found alive and well.

However, he could not in good conscience neglect Beatrice any longer.

What must she think about him abandoning her before she'd even regained consciousness?

Only Fletcher's reassurance that Beatrice's wound appeared worse than it was and she would make a full recovery persuaded Cassius to leave her side and hunt for Layton. After all, if it weren't for Cassius roping his brother into helping, Layton would not have gone missing.

He glanced upward.

The clear blue September sky and tranquil setting belied the battle within him. His mind warred between anticipating seeing Beatrice and despair about not finding his eldest brother.

Inhaling a deep breath to clear his thoughts, he opened the door without waiting for Simms, the butler.

Father had likely informed Beatrice that her uncle had orchestrated Layton's abduction.

How had she taken the news?

Not only had Fletcher already notified the magistrate of Highbury's involvement, but he had also delivered a letter from Father testifying to Highbury's guilt, which ensured the earl's arrest. The privileged sot wouldn't like life behind bars, but he'd abducted a powerful duke's son.

Highbury would face the consequences of his actions, peer or not.

A brisk tread on the black and white marble announced Simms' approach.

Sympathy crinkled the faithful servant's eyes at the corners.

"Lord Cassius, I've taken the liberty of ordering a bath and a tray for you."

How did the man even know Cassius had returned?

"Thank you." Cassius summoned an exhausted smile. "My parents? Miss Fairfax?"

Simms arranged his features into the neutral mien he reserved for guests.

Ah, so the butler knew something.

Something unpleasant.

"Your parents are in the duchess's private salon, Lord Cassius."

"Cassius?" Mother rushed into the foyer, her arms outstretched. "My dear, you are a frightful sight." She wrinkled her nose. "And you smell."

Nevertheless, she encircled him in a warm embrace.

Father followed in her wake, also hugging him. "Any word?"

Cassius didn't need to ask the duke to clarify.

He shook his head. "Lucian, Torrian, and Adolphus are following up on a lead in Hexham."

He scraped a hand through his gritty hair. God, he needed a good scrub. Preferably before he presented his odoriferous self to Beatrice, though with every breath, his heart yearned to see her sweet face.

"Hexham?" Father furrowed his forehead, obviously puzzled. "But we found his abductors hiding out in Penrith."

"True, but we came across a man from Corbridge who vows he saw a man matching Layton's description in Hexham. Corbridge and Hexham are only four miles apart."

Not a long distance, even on foot.

Cassius cast his mother a guarded glance. "He was hurt, Mother, but we don't know the extent of his injuries."

The color drained from her face, but she maintained her composure. "At least Highbury and his thugs have been apprehended. Fletcher should be back any time with news from London about Highbury's arrest."

In debt up to his starched neckcloth and owing ruthless money lenders a small fortune, Highbury had resorted to abduction and extortion.

Cassius gave a distracted nod. "Please tell Beatrice I'll come to see her as soon as I've made myself presentable."

Father cleared his throat. "Son...Miss Fairfax left two hours ago. I allowed her the use of the coach."

"*Left*?" Cassius repeated stupidly, his mind unable to comprehend Beatrice wasn't here waiting for him. "She isn't here?"

His parents shook their heads.

Beatrice had left.

She was gone.

Because she felt responsible for her uncle orchestrating Layton's abduction?

No, no, no.

Despair like he'd never known overwhelmed Cassius, and it was all he could do not to bend over and keen in agony. Constanza's betrayal had been a bee sting compared to this anguish.

Her green eyes brimming with worry, Mother squeezed his forearm. "She fretted the entire time she was here that she was an inconvenience and a burden. After the solicitors came—at her behest—and she signed the documents transferring her inheritance into her possession, she waited another week. When you didn't come home or write..."

His mother shrugged as if she didn't know what else to say. "Beatrice is an independent woman, and she is proud. Once she knew Highbury had been arrested, she told us she was leaving."

"We tried to convince her to stay." The sympathy in Father's gaze nearly undid Cassius.

He fought against the moisture stinging his eyes.

"But she knows her mind," Father said, "and nothing we said could persuade her."

"Where—" Cassius cleared his throat. "Where did

she go?"

Was that his voice?

That broken, tormented rasp?

"We don't know, darling." Mother exchanged a concerned glance with Father. "She said she had a few things to tend to before moving abroad."

Cassius jerked his head up.

He knew precisely where she would go first.

Beatrice would never abandon her beloved pets or Millborn.

He would bet everything he owned and never touch a paintbrush again if she wasn't on her way to Brighton.

Sprinting to the stairs, he called over his shoulder. "Father, have a fresh mount prepared and food I can take with me. Enough for Beatrice too, please."

"But Cassius, you've only just returned, and you are done in." His mother clasped her hands together. "Surely if you know where Beatrice is going, you can rest today and go after her tomorrow."

Already halfway up the stairs, Cassius shook his head. "No, Mother. I love her, and she shall know this day how very much."

"But—"

"Darling, don't waste your breath." Father draped an arm around his wife's shoulders. "He's in love."

Yes, I am.

Moreover, Cassius was almost giddy with joy.

He loved Beatrice.

Marvelous, unique, intrepid, kind Beatrice.

His father's chuckle followed Cassius down the corridor as he sprinted to his bedchamber.

After taking the fastest bath in the history of Hefferwickshire House and donning clean clothes in record time, Cassius bounded back down the stairs.

Simms and his parents waited for him in the foyer, along with Grandmama, Siobhan, and Aurelie.

Eyes shining with happiness and tears, Mother embraced him again. "Go fetch your Beatrice and bring her home."

"That gel is special, Cassius." Grandmama pulled him in for a fragrant hug amidst of chorus of tinkling bracelets and pendants. "I knew it the moment I laid eyes on her. And she is absolutely perfect for you."

"Indeed, she is." Only he'd been too blind, too self-absorbed and wallowing in self-pity to see how magnificent Beatrice was.

Stepping back, Grandmama cocked her head, reminding him of a little sparrow. "She's not taking the major route. Look for her where you've been before."

No one asked how Grandmama knew that bit of information. She had ways of knowing things that no one else did.

Still, her comment made no sense.

"What?" Cassius didn't know what she meant. "I don't..."

Look for her where you've been.

The Frolicking Fox.

He gave her a swift hug. "Thank you, Grandmama."

"I suppose this means there will be another wedding to plan." Mother didn't sound the least perturbed.

"If all goes well." Cassius couldn't contain his triumphant grin.

Simms handed him a small bundle. "Sustenance for your journey, Lord Cassius."

"Thank you." Cassius sprinted down the front stairs and leaped onto the saddled horse. Thank God, he could travel faster on horseback than Beatrice could by coach.

He meant to scold her soundly for not convalescing for another week or two and for traveling alone, although with the duchy's behemoth drivers, Farrel and Baldwin at the reins, Cassius was confident she was quite safe.

"I'm coming Beatrice Fairfax, and by heavens, I shall convince you to marry me."

TWENTY-SIX

On a less-traveled road to
The Frolicking Fox

THREE HOURS LATER

At the first glimpse of the Duke of Latham's coach grinding along the path in the distance, Cassius's blood quickened. His beloved Beatrice was in there, and soon he'd be able to take her in his arms and kiss her until she was breathless, profess how much he adored her, and beg her to accept his hand in marriage.

What a stupid lummox he'd been, refusing to allow himself to love her.

He whistled, and Baldwin glanced over his shoulder.

Grinning, the coachman waved and slowed the team to a gradual stop.

As Cassius approached, Beatrice and Nala poked their heads out the window. Craning to look up at the drivers, Beatrice shielded her eyes from the sun. "Why have we stopped?"

Baldwin jutted his chin in Cassius's direction, and Beatrice dutifully glanced down the roadway.

Nala woofed a canine greeting.

"*Cassius?*"

Wonder and perhaps a hint of doubt lit Beatrice's eyes.

The emerald green bonnet adorned with silk flowers and white feathers enhanced her glorious hair and eyes. A matching spencer with an intricate rose braid and undone silver buttons covered her slender shoulders.

God, she's lovely.

She'd either borrowed from the Westbrook women or, while she convalesced, had ordered a few garments and accouterments made. If the latter, knowing her as he did, Cassius would bet his studio, she had sewn a portion of her new wardrobe herself.

How Cassius had missed her.

His heart turned over, and joy he thought to never know again thrummed through him.

No, that wasn't true.

He had never been this happy—had never anticipated the future as much as he did now.

She scrunched her nose in that cute way she did when she was confused.

"Why are you here, Cassius?"

"You, Beatrice Fairfax, left without saying goodbye."

"*I'm* not the one who left without saying good-bye." More than a little heat laced her saucy retort. "You weren't even at Hefferwickshire House when I left. The same cannot be said of me when *you* departed."

Did a driver chuckle?

Cassius didn't spare them a glance to see which one.

It didn't matter if they thought him a besotted fool.

What mattered was the woman in the coach.

"And I regretted it every second I was away from you, which is why I am here now. To make amends."

She eyed him as one might a long-denied treasure—with yearning and wariness.

Distrust and hope.

He never took his focus off her as he dismounted, tied the mare to the back of the vehicle, and opened the coach door.

"Where to, Lord Cassius?"

Farrel didn't even pretend to hide his amusement.

"Home." Where Cassius and Beatrice would marry by special license as soon as feasible.

"Have I no voice in this decision?" Beatrice asked, clearly miffed.

Cassius placed a dusty boot on the step. "Of course you do."

She had no choice but to scoot over, which she did with admirable speed.

Once inside, he knocked on the roof and the coach slowly turned around.

Teddy and Nala wasted no time in greeting him with eager doggy kisses and wagging tails.

"I missed you too." Laughing, he nudged Nala aside so he could sit closer to Beatrice.

Lifting her nose with an Almack peeress's regal air, Beatrice regarded him cooly.

"I do not appreciate your highhandedness. I am on my way to Brighton. I have arrangements to make for Millborn and my animals."

"I suspected as much." He gathered her gloved hands into his. "But that can wait a few more days."

Her eyes grew round, and she released her breath in a rush. "Oh, I'm a selfish dolt. What news have you of Captain Westbrook?"

Cassius sighed. "We still haven't located him, but my brothers and cousin are following a strong lead."

"I feel responsible." Her eyes grew misty, and she dropped her chin to her chest. "Especially as we now know my uncle was behind his abduction."

"You did not cause any of this, Beatrice, and there is nothing you could have done to prevent it." Cassius nudged her chin upward until she met his eyes. "I missed you. Very much."

She formed a tremulous smile. "I missed you too."

He shook a finger at her.

"However, I'm not happy that you did not take a few more days to recover." Glancing at her emerald muslin-covered thigh, he asked, "You are healing well?"

"Yes. As you know, I was merely grazed. Fletcher's expertise in cleaning and stitching my wound no doubt also contributed to my swift recovery." She patted her leg. "I barely have any pain at all. Just if it's bumped, or if I move too quickly.

"I'm relieved to hear it." Cassius slipped an arm around her shoulders and when she didn't object, drew her nearer.

"Why did your brother give up practicing medicine?" Beatrice searched Cassius's face. "He's a talented doctor."

"That he is, but he couldn't abide the darker side of medicine. Specifically dealing with children dying." Cassius traced his fingers up and down her shoulder. "For all of Fletcher's outward sternness, he's a very compassionate man. It drove him to the bottle."

She laid her head on his shoulder, and if Cassius hadn't already given her his heart, it would have flopped at her feet. "It is heartbreaking when a patient dies, although mine are only animals."

He kissed the top of her head, and a feather tickled his

nose. "I believe people can love animals as much as humans."

"Cassius?"

"*Hmm?*" His eyelids grew heavier with each passing *clip-clop* of the horses' hooves.

"Why did you come after me?"

Leave it to Beatrice to get directly to the point.

With his forefinger, he turned her face so that she peered up at him.

"Because, Beatrice Fairfax, I love you and want to marry you."

He pressed his mouth to her forehead.

"Oh." She blinked, and a blush tinted her cheeks.

Oh?

"I thought when a man proposed, he kissed his intended on the mouth."

Cassius burst out laughing as he pulled her onto his lap. "I am more than happy to oblige you."

The first touch of his lips upon hers was the sweetest homecoming.

This, *this* was what love should be.

It was more than physical desire or lust. Love was the blending of two spirits, two souls finding completion in the other.

He teased the seam of her mouth until she opened the honeyed cavern to his gentle probing. Sighing, Beatrice looped her arms around his neck and kissed him back with an exuberance that made up for her inexperience.

The miles passed as he explored her mouth and gentle curves. Exhaustion and fatigue faded away under his growing ardor.

At last, Cassius reluctantly lifted his head.

Beatrice opened sultry, desire-filled eyes.

"Why did you stop?" Her siren's smile nearly undid him.

He eyed the opposite bench, mentally calculating how comfortable it would be to make her his in every way.

"I quite enjoyed kissing," she said.

"As did I, and that is why we must stop." He set her on the seat beside him and gave a pointed look at his hard groin. "When I make you mine, it will not be in a bumpy coach with two dogs watching."

"That would be a bit awkward." Beatrice giggled as she petted each dog. From beneath her lush lashes, she gave him a sideways, coy glance.

God help him resist the tempting armful that was Beatrice.

"I have a confession, Cassius."

He skewed an eyebrow upward. "Oh?"

"I vowed I'd get you to kiss me so that when I was an old, dried-up prune of a spinster and I couldn't sleep, I could recall that precious memory as I sat in my rocking chair, gazing at the moonlit, midnight sky with a couple of dogs curled at my feet.”

Emotion clogged Cassius's throat, and he grazed his fingertips over her cheek.

“We'll have a lifetime to make memories at midnight, my love.” He wiggled his eyebrows. “If you agree to marry me.”

Consternation suddenly gripped him.

What if she didn't love him as he did her?

“You do love me, Beatrice, don't you?”

She cupped his face with her palm.

“Yes, I love you, Cassius Westbrook. You've shown me that there are good men in the world, and I want to spend the rest of my life with you and only you.”

The breath left his lungs in a whoosh.

“Thank God.” He pressed his forehead against hers, relief flooding him.

“I do have a condition or two.” She leaned back, her eyes twinkling. “I want to continue rescuing animals.”

“Darling, you can have an entire menagerie.” He would have to give up his studio. There wasn't room for an animal hospital there. The idea didn't cause him undue concern. “Whatever makes you happy.”

“You, Lord Cassius Westbrook. You make me happy.” Smiling, she lifted her mouth to his. “Now kiss me again.”

EPILOGUE

Highbury House Estate

EARLY OCTOBER 1829

Humming a lullaby, Beatrice leaned over to smooth the downy black hair from her newborn son's forehead as he slept in his cradle in the nursery, one tiny fist above his head. And to think she believed she could have been content without children.

What a fool she had been.

Now, married just over a year, she couldn't imagine her life without Cassius or Antonius.

Cassius embraced her from behind, snaking his strong

arms around her waist as he whispered in her ear. "How is the little fellow?"

Turning her head, she kissed his firm jaw. "Sleeping, but who knows for how long?"

Only a week old, the babe had yet to settle into a schedule.

Millborn trundled in, followed by the nursemaid, Pendle.

"I'll watch the little tyke," Beatrice's old companion said. "Go get yourselves a bit of breakfast. I'll let you know if he awakens."

Now that Millborn had officially retired, most of Antonius's care fell to Pendle, but the elderly servant enjoyed rocking the infant. As she had no kin of her own, the elderly servant would likely spend the rest of her days in Beatrice's household.

"Thank you, Millborn."

Even after knowing her most of her life, the servant still wouldn't let Beatrice address the woman by her first name.

"It wouldn't be proper," Millborn maintained.

All those months ago, Cassius's friend, Dr. Lancaster, had insisted on moving Millborn from Highbury House to the Royal Sussex County Hospital—against Uncle Cedric's adamant protestations. Had he not done so, Dr. Lancaster vowed she would have perished.

Through Cassius's cousin Torrian's clever sleuthing,

they had learned that Beatrice's fiend of an uncle had plotted to bribe a knave to marry her in a phony ceremony. Then when she died from an "accident" shortly after being wed, the truth would come forth that she was never really married.

Torrian hadn't revealed precisely how he had encouraged Dungworth to reveal those salacious tidbits. Since she had no offspring, Cedric intended to claim her fortune.

A twisted, perverse, and desperate scheme by a twisted, perverse, and desperate man.

Charged with abduction, extortion, intent to commit fraud, conspiracy to commit murder, and half a dozen other crimes, Uncle Cedric hadn't escaped incarceration. Plus, his lack of funds prevented him from bribing his way out of his sentence.

Not that he stood a snowflake's chance in Hades of avoiding his fate. Not when he'd made a mortal enemy of the powerful, influential, and popular Duke of Latham.

Uncle Cedric had died a mere six months later—infection from a rat bite.

A most deserving end.

It seemed the earldom's coffers were empty as a beggar's purse, which explained the new Earl of Highbury selling unentailed properties, including Highbury House. Why Uncle Cedric hadn't done the same, Beatrice couldn't fathom. Except he'd always been a prideful man, and if he sold his houses, others would soon know he wasn't as wealthy as he pretended.

Uncle Cedric hadn't been above pawning the earldom's jewels, however, and had paste replicas made. Even the emeralds she'd worn for her portrait that first day turned out to be fake.

The new earl wasn't the least pleased when he learned of Uncle's perfidy.

What caused a despicable excuse for humanity to refuse to sell his properties to avoid the poorhouse, but would contemplate murdering his niece for her fortune?

When Beatrice learned her childhood home was on the market, she and Cassius decided it would be the perfect place for her menagerie—cared for by Hans—and an upper-story solar made a spectacular art studio.

"How are you feeling, my love?" Cassius twined an arm around Beatrice's still slightly thick waist as they walked to the breakfast room.

Nala and Teddy refused to budge from the nursery since Antonius's arrival except to do their business outside with the utmost haste before dashing back inside to guard the infant.

Beatrice closed her eyes. "Tired, but blissfully happy."

"BeBe, are you certain you should travel to Hefferwickshire House at the end of November?" Worry creased the corners of Cassius's indigo eyes. "Your lying-in period will scarcely have ended, and I don't want you overtaxed."

"Cassius Westbrook, don't you know by now, I am not a fragile flower?" Her loving smile belied her mock sternness.

"No, you, my love, are a canna lily. Resilient and strong, and incredibly beautiful." He chuckled and pulled her near to kiss her temple. "I suppose we must go. Grandmama did beckon."

"And Layton and Lilly are expecting their first child," she said.

Now that was a romantic tale of its own.

As Beatrice and Cassius passed the drawing room, she glimpsed her portrait hanging above the fireplace.

A confident, poised woman gazed back at her.

How had Cassius captured those elements when Beatrice hadn't been the least bit confident or poised at the time?

She paused, and Cassius followed her gaze.

"I knew you would be a marvel on canvas," he said, as though reading her mind.

Beatrice rolled her eyes, adoring how much he cherished her. "Your love makes you biased."

"Your modesty, dear wife, becomes you, but the British Institution does not award five hundred pounds for excellence in art unless the piece is truly exceptional, especially considering my submission wasn't a history or a landscape painting."

They continued on their way.

How very different this house had become, now that love and laughter filled it.

She rested her head against her husband's shoulder, loving him so much, her heart overflowed.

"I'm so glad you accepted the commission to paint me, Cassius. We might never have met otherwise."

"I believe we would have met another way, my love." Cassius turned her into his embrace. "We were destined to be together."

He lowered his mouth to hers, and Beatrice gave herself over to the joy and bliss of his kiss.

I hope you enjoyed
MEMORIES MADE AT MIDNIGHT
and following the romantic journey
of Cassius and Beatrice.
If you'd like to leave a review please
scan the following QR Code.

SCAN HERE TO LEAVE A REVIEW FOR
"MEMORIES MADE AT MIDNIGHT"

FROM THE DESK OF COLLETTE CAMERON®

Cassius had been hounding me to write his story, but I hadn't decided who would make the perfect heroine for him. She needed to be as unique as his twin's sweetheart, but someone he would risk his broken heart for. And she needed to need him, even if she didn't know it.

I've mentioned before how tough life was for women, historically. They had few rights, including keeping possession of money they had or inherited. However, women ensured they gained small measures of power.

They accomplished this by incorporating specific stipulations and provisions on how funds they bequeathed could be used. This allowed some women to retain control and prevented husbands from doing what they wished with their wife's money.

In an era when women were expected to marry and

have children, Beatrice was an anomaly. Not that every woman who wanted to marry had the chance. A woman without a dowry might never have the opportunity.

While St. Nicholas Church was the main parish church in Brighton in 1828, Reverend Ellison Dawkins was not its cleric. His character is purely fictional. The British Institution really existed and focused on supporting talented authors. The Royal Sussex County Hospital was one of the first hospitals in the area.

It would have been scandalous in the extreme for Beatrice to travel unchaperoned with a man, but history is full of women taking risks and cocking a snook at society. I applaud her daring and hope you do too.

One other point of interest I'd like to address is the various herbs and plants I mentioned that have medicinal properties. I researched each of the natural remedies, and while they have been used for the purposes I mentioned, I am not a doctor and do not suggest anyone use the herbs in the manner I have described. You should always consult a physician before taking any supplements.

I hope you enjoyed Cassius and Beatrice's story.

Layton and Lilly's will wrap up the Chronicles of the Westbrook Brides Series.

Hugs,

Collette Cameron®

GIGGLES ARE GUARANTEED
COLLETTE'S CHERIS READER GROUP

If you love to chat about all things romance-book related and enjoy taking part in fun and engaging live events, contests, and giveaways join **Collette's Chèris VIP Reader Group,** my exclusive private book group on Facebook.

Giggles are guaranteed!

Hope to see you there,

Collette Cameron®

Please scan the following QR Code to join:

ALSO BY COLLETTE CAMERON®
BLUE ROSE ROMANCE® LLC

COLLETTE CAMERON'S®

COMPLETE BOOK LIST

CHRONICLES OF THE WESTBROOK BRIDES

A Romantic Opposites Attract Mystery & Suspense

Family Saga Regency Romance

Moonlight Wishes and Midnight Kisses — Bonus Novella

Midnight Christmas Waltz — Book 1

Mission at Midnight — Book 2

The Midnight Marquess — Book 3

Holly, Mistletoe, and Midnight Snow — Book 4

The Wallflower's Midnight Waltz— Book 5

Minuet at Midnight— Book 6

Kiss a Rake at Midnight — Book 7

Unmasked at Midnight — Book 8

DUKES COME CALLING

A Sensual Marriage of Convenience

Regency Historical Romance

FOR THE LOVE OF AN EARL (Wicked Earls' Club)

A Humorous Aristocrat and Wallflower

Regency Romance Adventure

Earl of Wainthorpe — Book 1

Earl of Scarborough — Book 2

Earl of Keyworth — Book 3

Earl of Renshaw — Book 4

HEART OF A SCOT

A Passionate Enemies to Lovers

Scottish Highlander Historical Mystery

Romance Adventure

To Love a Highland Laird — Book 1

To Redeem a Highland Rogue — Book 2

To Seduce a Highland Scoundrel — Book 3

To Woo a Highland Warrior — Book 4

To Enchant a Highland Earl — Book 5

To Defy a Highland Duke — Book 6

To Marry a Highland Marauder — Book 7

To Bargain with a Highland Buccaneer — Book 8

A Christmas Kiss for the Highlander — Book 9

HIGHLAND HEATHER ROMANCING A SCOT: CASTLE BRIDES

A Passionate Enemies to Lovers Second Chance Scottish Highlander Mystery Romance

Heart of a Highlander — Prequel

The Viscount's Vow — Book 1

The Highlander's Heiress — Book 2

The Earl's Enticement — Book 3

Triumph and Treasure — Book 4

Virtue and Valor — Book 5

Heartbreak and Honor — Book 6

Scandal's Splendor — Book 7

Passion and Plunder — Book 8

SECRETS OF SCANDALOUS LADIES
A Romantic Class Difference Forced Proximity

Regency Romance with Aristocrats

THE CULPEPPER MISSES
A Humorous Wallflower Family Saga

Regency Romantic Comedy

The Earl and the Spinster — Book 1

The Marquis and the Vixen — Book 2

The Lord and the Wallflower — Book 3

The Buccaneer and the Bluestocking — Book 4

The Lieutenant and the Lady — Book 5

THE HONORABLE ROGUES®
A Second Chance Redeemable Rogue
and Wallflower Regency Romance

A Kiss for a Rogue — Book 1

A Bride for a Rogue — Book 2

A Rogue's Scandalous Wish — Book 3

To Capture a Rogue's Heart — Book 4

The Rogue and the Wallflower — Book 5

A Rose for a Rogue — Book 6

'Twas the Rogue Before Christmas — Book 7

A Rogue Worth the Risk — Book 8

ABOUT THE AUTHOR
COLLETTE CAMERON®

USA Today Bestselling author Collette Cameron® is renowned for her captivating, humorous, and heart-warming Scottish and Regency historical romance novels. With over 65 published titles, over 1.4 million books sold around the world, and multiple writing awards to her credit, Collette is a well-known author in the world of historical romance. Readers love her witty and relatable characters including daring rogues, dashing scoundrels, and the strong and spirited heroines who capture their hearts. From the rugged highlands to the refined drawing rooms of Regency England, Collette's novels will transport you to another time and place, where love and adventure are just a page away.

Collette's Sweet-to-Spicy Timeless Romances® are the perfect escape for readers looking for romantic escape, poignant inspiration, engaging humor, and entertaining stories.

Based in the Pacific Northwest, Collette is surrounded by the lush greenery and rainy skies that inspire her writing. She dreams of one day splitting her time between the Pacific Northwest and Scotland. In the meantime, she indulges in her love of all things cobalt blue, dachshunds, chocolate, and of course, crafting her next historical romance.

Blue Rose Romance® LLC
PO Box 167
Scappoose, Oregon 97056 USA
collettecameron.com

If you haven't joined Collette's exclusive mailing list scan the foliing QR Code to sign up!
You'll get access to exclusive content, sneak peeks,
contests, giveaways, and more...
(P.S. No spammy stuff.)

THE REGENCY ROSE® VIP CLUB

Follow Collette on social media.
Scan the following QR Code:

collettecameron.com

www.ingramcontent.com/pod-product-compliance
Lightning Source LLC
Chambersburg PA
CBHW052026220726
48293CB00015B/325